THE WEBBING BOW

THE SECOND CRYSTAL KINGDOM NOVEL

RAYMOND S FLEX

1

THE MAGICAL COUNCIL

MA'REYGAR felt his muscles groan and creak as he lumbered his way up the stone staircase. He could smell the fresh mountain air, and the tingle of the chill on his tongue as he climbed higher and higher. All that sounded up there was the steady *tap* his cane made on contact with the stone slabs beneath his feet.

He paused on the stairs and peered up above him, into the swirling fog, and the lightly falling snow. He felt a shudder pass through him, so strong as to almost rattle his bones. His teeth chattered until he could taste the enamel on his tongue.

Here he was, in the midst of the Sable Mountains. He had come far, spent a lot of strife, and now he was almost there.

Almost at the Magical Council.

But still a little way to go.

The soles of Ma'reygar's feet were the only part of his body that seemed to carry any warmth. Somewhat ironic for a fire mage.

And the soles of his feet felt as if he'd trod across miles and miles of hot coals.

And now the blisters were bursting.

He watched his breath form clouds before his face, and he tried to make out his destination, the enormous great castle built up here. Where the seat of the Magical Council was located.

But he could see nothing but fog, and snow in the fading light.

He hadn't much time to waste.

He could quite easily freeze to death out here on this exposed staircase.

And so, with that thought in mind, that thought of *death* that had been on his mind so much lately, he forced his knotted muscles forwards, and commanded his feet on.

Just one step at a time.

Off in the distance, he could hear the mountain wind bustling up, gathering its strength, and whistling through the unseen valleys. From the little time he'd spent up in the Mountains, and he never attempted to spend longer than necessary here, he knew that the wind picked up something fierce in the evenings.

And he had experienced that again, just from this trek, from camping out on his way to the Magical Council.

But it was one thing for him to pick out a sheltered piece of terrain, when up here, on these stairs, the truth was that he was exposed to all the elements.

On either side of him he saw the enormous, gut-churning drops . . . or at least he knew they were there, because the fog wouldn't allow him to see them right now.

He tightened his grasp on his staff, feeling his fingertips find the worn-down notches he'd worked into the wood after all these years. And he felt his heart swell a little in his chest, and his pulse race. He knew that his body . . . the fire magic within him . . . was doing battle with this frosty gale. And, after all these days of his journey, after all this effort he'd put into getting here, to the seat of the Magical Council, he knew that he had only had so much resistance left within him.

Tap. Shuffle-shuffle.

Tap. Shuffle-shuffle.

Beyond the wailing breeze, Ma'reygar picked out his own sounds. The *tap* of his staff, followed by the shuffle of his shoes against the stone staircase. And his heart played percussion too.

Thump-thump.

Thump.

Thump-thump.

Thump.

He tried to make those sounds into his superiors, driving him forwards, driving him onwards up further towards his destination.

Thump-thump.

Tap.

Thump.

Shuffle-shuffle.

Thump-thump.

A stiffer wind blew, and this time it carried a bite.

Hail rained down on Ma'reygar, pattering indifferently hard down on him. Ma'reygar's meagre cloak provided insufficient shelter to the onslaught, and he felt those tiny, freezing-cold shards beat against his skin.

Chill his blood.

Ma'reygar pressed his lips tight together, and squinted once more through the fading light. Of course he could try a spell, summon fire in the palm of his hands. But he might just as easily topple over from trying.

He wasn't a man of thirty any longer.

He was well into his fiftieth year.

And getting older every day.

Ma'reygar knew that he had to conserve strength, if for nothing else, then for the return journey. And if he failed then it might well be in vain. Just thinking about it sent a shudder scurrying down his spine, and turned him sick to the stomach.

Because he was determined that he *would* be successful.

They *wouldn't* turn *him* away.

And then the wind blew in at him harder still.

Ma'reygar clutched his cloak around him, and buried his face into the frayed, half-frozen wool. But it provided no comfort.

The wind kept on blowing, and the hail grew heavier.

The hail fell harder.

And harder still.

Soon Ma'reygar could hardly breathe for the hail striking him so hard. He listened to it patter off the stone steps all around him, and it filled his hearing . . . filled his *skull*. And he was sure that he was screaming, that he could feel his lungs burning.

Just when he thought he could take no more, he felt the hail subside.

The wind drop.

And then he heard a low, familiar, and not unwelcome voice. "Ma'reygar, please, come inside. You must've had a frantic journey."

Ma'reygar had no need to unburrow his face from his cloak to know who the voice belonged to. Not just the one of the appointed seven members of the Magical Council, but the head of the Magical Council himself.

The most fearsome, and feared, ice mage in all the world.

Or so some said.

Yunt'ga'boar.

The entrance hall of the Magical Council was warm, and smelled sweat.

Of honey.

Through the large door which looked into the feasting halls, Ma'reygar could see a pig roasting on a spit. He breathed in the thick scent of it floating on the otherwise musky air. And he could smell a balance of ash and frost equally there.

Or was there just a little more frost than ash?

Yunt'ga'boar led the way.

He wore a plush, velvety cloak, with a crimson sash tied at his waist. And he walked with a sort of mince to his step, as if he was floating on a cloud.

Or as if he was carried by an invisible fog.

Ma'reygar felt his senses restoring themselves, and the *thrum* of his heart return to its normal, gentle rhythm. He looked to the spiral staircase, up which Yunt'ga'boar was headed, holding tightly to the oak banister.

Yunt'ga'boar addressed Ma'reygar without turning round. "If you'd sent a messenger then perhaps we might've had someone meet you further back along the track. We could've had a mule sent for you to help you up the stairs."

Ma'reygar felt that Yunt'ga'boar's words carried a slight to them. "I managed quite all right on my own."

Yunt'ga'boar turned and gave Ma'reygar a wry smile. "Yes, I can see that you did."

Looking into Yunt'ga'boar's soot-black eyes, into those lifeless, matted irises, always made him feel uneasy. Thankfully, mercifully, Yunt'ga'boar turned back around and continued on his way.

Ma'reygar felt a lump forming in his throat, and he swallowed it back. "I'd like to see the Council before I think about resting, if that's all right with you."

Yunt'ga'boar halted, mid-step. "The Council?" he said, his words echoing around the entrance hall down below.

"Yes," Ma'reygar said. "I've a proposal for them."

"A proposal you say?" Yunt'ga'boar said, that same smile trailing over his lips. "And what sort of a *proposal* would that be?"

Ma'reygar waited. He didn't want to show all his cards so early on. He needed time. He *wanted* time. Once he had all the mages assembled, all seven of them, then he would reveal his plans. It was a Council for a reason, however much Yunt'ga'boar would like to see himself as the outright leader.

Some sort of *king* of the magical community because of his status as Head Chair.

A position which might just as easily have been Ma'reygar's, if they'd lived in different times.

Ma'reygar studied Yunt'ga'boar's profile, saw all those wrinkles unfolding in that leathery face of his, and then, slowly, and with apparent great deliberation, Yunt'ga'boar said, "Fine. I shall have them assemble at once."

Although Ma'reygar felt his fatigue causing him to tremble, making his voice shake as he spoke, he knew that he had to make his proposal clear as soon as possible. Later on, when he had his answer, then would be the time to tuck into that succulent-looking roast pig.

The room, the meeting hall, was thick with pipe smoke, and he could hear hail rattling down outside, against the windowpanes.

He knew that most likely that was of Yunt'ga'boar's conjuring, but he wouldn't allow that to deter him.

Conversation babbled about the high-ceilinged meeting room, rendering all the conversations just as inaudible as each other. At least from where Ma'reygar sat, at the head of the enormous, oblong table, and opposite Yunt'ga'boar.

He traced the bluish twirls of pipe smoke as they puffed up into the air, from the pipes of the assembled mages, and he took them all in, looked them all over, comparing them with his memories of them, how he *remembered* them looking in his mind's eye.

And he couldn't help thinking to himself that everyone looked much *older*.

There were six other members of the Magical Council. Three fire and three ice, as was the custom. With Yunt'ga'boar as the head of the Council, that meant that ice magic outweighed fire by four to three.

But Ma'reygar refused to allow that to deter him either.

He had come here to deliver his proposal, and the Magical Council, if nothing else, would hear him out.

He breathed in the thick smoke, felt it prickle his lungs, and it was good. It put him back in touch with his fire magic, reassured him that although he faced down four ice mages here before him, including the one who many mages would consider to be the most powerful of their times—Yunt'ga'boar—he could stand up to them all.

He was almost certain that he could smell, almost *taste*, that roasting pig, its scent wafting into the meeting hall on the draught.

He so wanted to take a bite.

Soon, soon.

Ma'reygar cleared his throat and got up to his feet, helping himself up with the aid of the back of the hefty, oak chair. He looked out over the mages, and waited, patiently, for them to notice him standing up there.

For them to finish their conversations in their own time.

He waited another second, savouring the silent moments, and feeling the hairs stick up at the back of his neck. He clasped hold of the back of the oak chair and dug his fingertips into the swirling designs.

"Brothers and sisters," Ma'reygar began, "I've come here before you to serve you with a proposal. And, please, I beg of you that you do not think this is something I've been thinking on lightly, but, for what it is, a matter of great importance."

He drew breath, looked round the room, and forced himself to meet every one of the mages' eyes.

Save Yunt'ga'boar.

He couldn't face gazing into *those* eyes twice in one day.

"We live in changing times, *turbulent* times, which is to say that the magical and mortal realms are tottering on the brink of war."

Over in the corner of the room, he heard one of the mages mutter something to their neighbour. When Ma'reygar looked in the mage's direction, she stopped immediately, and turned back to him with a slight, almost friendly, smile, waiting patiently for him to continue.

Grendlin.

That was her name.

A fire mage, like him.

Ma'reygar continued, feeling the confidence flowing more easily now. Feeling the twitch of his magic restoring itself to his veins, tickling him from the inside with its reassuring glow.

"And it falls to us, the magical, to decide just how the battle will play out." Ma'reygar held up his hand. "For so long we've been exiled here, to the Sable Mountains. *Tolerated*. Meanwhile the king's army, led by Herimyre, traipse through the land gaoling mages that stray into the Kingdom of Shellacnass. And we, up here, safe in our mountain spot, would like to think, to believe, that Herimyre has finished his quest. That he has won his victory."

Ma'reygar glared round the room once again, meeting all the mages' eyes. And this time, feeling the confidence flowing a little stronger through him, he managed to look Yunt'ga'boar in the eye. And then he continued:

"And I stand here, before you today, to tell you that Herimyre has no such intention of stopping there. That I have been privy to all his plans, to his wishes and desires, that I have it on the best authority that he wants to strike out into the rest of 'his' kingdom, and truly banish magic from Shellacnass forever more."

Muttering broke out all around the table now.

Ma'reygar allowed himself the sliver of a smile. This was just what he had wanted. He had wanted panic, a sense of anger, and, most of all, fear.

In his mind, Ma'reygar had nothing but contempt for these mages up here, for the so-called Magical Council. They sat up here in the Sable Mountains, in their relative safety, like a bunch of hibernating bears. They *needed* someone to shift them.

Even if that someone was creative with the truth.

Because Ma'reygar knew that the last thing on Herimyre's mind was to march into the Sable Mountains and have mound upon mound of soldiers slaughtered by the hands of fire and ice.

No, Herimyre was much too intelligent.

But the Magical Council didn't know that.

They relied on whispers and rumour.

And, sometimes, like now, *lies*.

Ma'reygar watched the befuddlement wreak havoc on the crowd before him, on those apparent masters of fire and ice in equal measure. The only one who remained stoic, composed, straight-backed and staring right at Ma'reygar, was, of course, Yunt'ga'boar.

And Ma'reygar could almost feel the frostiness of that glare freezing his blood.

A few moments later, Yunt'ga'boar called the hall to order, and then he looked to Ma'reygar. His voice, just like before, was low, almost devoid of emotion. And his expression was colourless as the ice which he could summon from his fingertips.

"And so, what is your proposal?" he said.

Ma'reygar felt the roaring fire in his gut, matched with the fatigue of his muscles. And yet he kept himself under control, and his voice sure and proud.

"I propose a vote on assembling a party to snatch the throne from out under the king's backside."

Yunt'ga'boar remained totally still, his gaze unmoving from Ma'reygar's, and he laid both his palms flat on the table. This was the moment of truth. Yunt'ga'boar could approve or deny the request.

Could Yunt'ga'boar see that Ma'reygar was being creative with his information, could he see that he might have something at stake in this, that he might be *burning* for revenge?

Yunt'ga'boar pursed his lips, and when he spoke his words uncoiled like a frosty gale. "Very well," he said. "We shall put it to a vote." He paused for a long time, deep in thought, and then added, "Although, it sounds to me that we shall need much more than a party. We shall need an army."

And in that moment, Ma'reygar was sure that he could feel all the ice that lingered in his veins, that hung over him, melt away.

And his mind switch to practical matters.

2

MURDER

LOUSON DORF'S hand gripped the handle of the Webbing Blade tight. He was surrounded by darkness. He could hear the breathing. And he could make out the shape of the sleeping man. In his bed.

The man he knew to be the king.

The King of Shellacnass.

The chill from the Webbing Blade clambered up his arm, and jangled through his veins. He could almost feel it freezing his bones. When he breathed in he smelled several different scents. Mountain herbs, perhaps. Or something that, having been a working hand, a simple farm worker, he had never had the chance to smell before.

His heart throbbed in his chest, and he felt it rising up to the base of his throat. He wanted to calm himself down, but most of all he wanted to be out of here.

He wanted this deed done.

Once and for all.

But first he had to do it.

He had to kill.

Lou crunched his teeth together and focussed on his target, on that chest rising and falling, and he stalked closer.

Outside the window, over his shoulder, he heard an owl hoot.

He froze. And he analysed the sound a few moments.

It wasn't the crow call, the *ca-kaw* he'd agreed with Hildie.

As he lurked there, bathed in the gloom, he almost wished that it had been the crow call, that she was going to put him out of his misery.

Let him escape without having *killed*.

He turned his attention back to the sleeping man. The man who he called king.

He trod on another couple of steps, and then realised he could go no further. The king's soft mattress now pressed up against his knee, and now he stood directly over the sleeping man. And he grasped the Webbing Blade tighter, felt its chill burn his bare skin.

He stared at the sleeping man's face, took in the sturdy features, the proud, thick nose, and the heavy lips. And the slightly soft skin that revealed the man not to have spent all that much time out in the sun.

Unlike Lou, and his fellow working hands.

Or even like the Royal Guards who trod the battlements.

Lou's heart skipped several beats, and his hands shook, but he saw them, out before him, almost detached from his body, the Webbing Blade grasped between both of them. And then. Just like that. He brought the Webbing Blade down with a mighty thrust.

Right into the king's chest.

Everything slowed down. Lou could suddenly hear the slight twitching of a branch outside his window, a bird landing on it, and, a little further off, he heard the howl of a wolf, and then, much closer, he could even hear the scuttle of the ants across the floor of the king's chambers, as they ran over Lou's boots.

He peered down at them, through the darkness, watched them pour over the toe of his boot, all of them busy, all of them rushing to get somewhere. As if afraid of disturbing them, he tapped his boot a couple of times, and watched a few of them bounce off.

Slip out of sight beneath the king's bed.

And then he looked back to the king, saw him there, in his bed, his eyes still clasped tight, and the Webbing Blade buried in his chest. He made no sound. He kept breathing. It was as if the dagger hadn't had any impact on him whatsoever.

Like the king's chest had merely been thin air.

Slowly, Lou looked up, over the prostrate king, and into the shadows, into the corner of the room. And standing there he saw another man. A brisk and upright man. And he wore a strong sword down at his side, his hand resting on the hilt.

Why wouldn't he charge Lou?

Wasn't he here to protect the king?

Would he just stand by and watch on?

Then Lou looked back to the king, to the Webbing Blade jutting out from his chest, and, in a single, swift movement, he tore it out from the king's chest, as easily as if he'd merely been slipping the dagger blade out of a block of cheese, and he rushed for the window behind him.

Lou hoisted himself up onto the window ledge, slipping several times, but finally getting a hold on his foundation. And only then did he dare a glance back over his shoulder, to the man standing off in the corner of the room. The man who just stood by and watched him.

The man that Lou knew was called Herimyre.

Captain of the Royal Guards.

The king slept on, apparently unmoved. There was no wound in his chest, no bloodied bed sheets, and he breathed in and out with a calm . . . *kingly* grace.

Lou turned back to the window, to the outside, to the palace gardens lying below him. And then he looked to his side, to the tree where he saw a large crow perched on the branch staring at him.

Its feathers were pit-black, and its eyes like a pair of highly polished marbles gleaning in the moonlight. And it held onto its branch tight with its talons.

It wasn't a *cursed* crow.

No.

It didn't have the bright red eyes of the cursed animals.

But its beak seemed to grind back and forth as if chewing on something, and its feathers ruffled in the gentle morning breeze.

Lou looked down again, to the palace gardens, to the soft grass below him.

He knew that if he fell from here he would surely die.

And yet, inexplicably and inevitably, he felt his weight tipping forwards, and his arms sprawling, and his feet leaving the ledge.

And he fell and fell.

He kept falling until it seemed he'd never hit the bottom. He lost himself in the waft of air all around him, he felt it blowing his hair over his face, and snapping his cloak tight to his frame. And then he heard a muffled voice, a gentle voice.

"Lou? Lou?"

Somehow he recognised the voice, but, at the same time, he couldn't place it in his mind. His mind could only see the sprawling darkness before him. The great, bottomless pit opening up below.

And as he felt himself falling into the abyss, he squeezed the handle of the Webbing Blade all the tighter, and held it to his chest.

"Lou? . . ."

3

AWAKE

"...Lou!"

This time there was a sharpness to the call of his name, and Lou snapped to. He blinked the sleep from his eyes, and was all at once pounded by the same darkness all around him. That same darkness from the king's quarters.

His mind escaped him.

He got caught in a flurry of thought.

Slowly the details came back to him.

The smell of pine wood. His dried-up mouth. The sigh of wind through the trees. The softness beneath him. He reached out his hand. Grass. Long grass. That was what he lay on.

And then he peered up.

"Lou?"

It was his sis, Syre.

Lou blinked away yet more sleep, and he seemed to get a better handle on the darkness surrounding him. It didn't seem so complete as it had done before. He could make out the shapes around him, and his sis's face staring down at him.

The Moon shone through the leaves of the forest and set everything in a midnight glow.

Lou's skull ached, and every muscle in his body felt tight. And he was absolutely parched. He reached up and massaged his temples with his fingers, and that helped a little.

At least it seemed to ease the constant rush of blood.

He blinked some more, still trying to brush off the daze, and only then did he realise that Syre was holding out a canister to him.

Water.

When he reached out, he saw that his hand was shaking . . . and then, he looked to his other hand.

He saw that it was pressed up against his chest, and that he held the Webbing Blade there. All of a sudden he felt its chill, and the prickle of its ice magic burrowing holes into him. He clasped his eyes shut as he tore it away from him and dropped it into the long grass beside him.

The chill left him. And he got that bitter-sweet sensation of control returning to him. As if he was returning to the mortal realm. This was just what Hildie had taught him to expect as he got better control of his powers.

As he learned to understand them.

He almost tore the canister from his sis's hand and he held the sprout to his lips and drank it all down. He felt the water brush past his tongue and slide straight down his throat. He wiped his lips with the back of the sleeve of his tunic, and then handed the canister back to Syre, and said, "Is there a stream nearby? I'm thirsty as a horse."

Syre shook her head, and the moonbeams bounced over her

tangled hair. She brushed a lock of hair back behind her ears, and then flinched at some sound in the distance. When she spoke again her speech was hurried. And there was the snap of urgency in the air.

"I woke you because I saw them—back along the path."

For a few seconds Lou was completely lost. His mind was still occupied with the dream, with the killing of the king, of Herimyre standing in the corner of the room, doing nothing. And with the crow outside the window.

He wished he could share it with Hildie.

Perhaps when they got back to the encampments she would be there.

But he knew that was only vague hoping.

Lou stumbled up onto his feet and looked about, to their temporary camp out here in the woods. Their things all gathered into a single, wrapped-up, mud-stained bindle. All their food. Their horses remained tied up a few paces away, off in another clearing.

Both of them swayed slightly in their sleep.

He wondered whether horses had nightmares too.

He saw just where Syre had been sleeping, the blanket she'd laid down over the long grass, and then the hard-bound book she kept with her, that she'd wrapped up in her change of clothes and used as a pillow. He didn't need to see the title to know the words etched onto its cover:

A Practical Understanding of Dark Magic.

They were camping out because that morning they had got information from a hobblesman passing through the encampment, on his way to the Sable Mountains. He had told them about the procession of Royal Guards that was passing along the trail, of the gaol cart that they lugged along between them.

And that the hobblesman had seen a pair of men in the ragged remnants of pitch-black skuller uniforms, behind the bars.

Lou had known instantly that those two men were Sully and Rut. His friends. The ones that they'd been forced to leave behind when they'd fled from Ilsnare.

When Lou had *killed* the king.

The hobblesman had told them that he'd stopped to speak with the Royal Guards a while, that he'd sold them some of his herbs, and they'd confided in him that they were headed for the port of Shildersmoore, and that the two men were headed for the prison colony of Onderswort.

Just that name had sent shudders down Lou's spine, and his gut to jelly. Every child in the Kingdom of Shellacnass knew about Onderswort. Onderswort was the word that every parent brought up whenever they wished to reach for the mightiest threat in their arsenal.

And still to this day it affected Lou.

He had heard the stories, of the town right on the brink of the kingdom, the sad place where they worked the people from dusk to dawn so that they never saw the sunlight.

For Lou, a working hand accustomed to being out in the fields, to being warmed by the sun's rays, it seemed like the greatest of punishments.

Too great of a punishment.

And that was where Sully and Rut were headed.

Lou picked his way through the camp, and between the trees. He felt a few branches scrape up against the exposed skin at his arms, but he didn't break his stride. He could hear Syre crunching through the undergrowth behind him, but he didn't dare turn his head from what was happening in front of him.

He guided his way through another few trees so that he was at the fringes of the forest, and then he looked out through the pine needles, and onto the plains.

The plains were lit up as brightly in the moonlight as they might've been at midday.

Off in the distance he could see the procession approaching. He counted five, no six, mounted horsemen, and then the gaoler's cart, driven by two horses, and a guard sitting up on the driver's seat.

Eight horses all together.

Seven guards in all.

The gaoler's cart rocked from side to side as it crunched over the path, making steady progress along the plains.

Lou guessed that within twenty minutes or so the cart would be level with them. And by then he would have to be ready.

He glanced back over his shoulder, to Syre standing there, her mouth agape. He had tried to make her stay at the encampment but she had refused.

Flat refused him.

And when he had tried to frighten her, it had seemed only to make her more intent on coming along with him. And so here she was.

Here *they* were.

But now he was intent that this was as far as she would get. He spoke to her briskly, and concisely, as he marched back towards their camp, turning his back on the approaching procession, and the gaoler's cart carrying his two friends. "You are to stay here. At the camp. Whatever happens. If they strike me down, if . . . something does happen, then you're to take one of the horses and gallop away. Is that clear?"

She was silent on his heels.

He halted his retreat to the camp, and he wheeled around,

finding himself nose to nose with her. He saw the fright in her eyes, the slight quivering of her lips, and he knew it had been a great mistake not to have been more firm.

To have made her see sense.

To have forced her to stay behind at the encampments.

"Is that clear?"

"Yes," she said, her answer almost a whimper.

"Good," Lou said, striding through the camp, and over to the tuft of long grass, now flattened from where he'd been sleeping.

He crouched down, dug around in the grass, and located the Webbing Blade, still lying there, just where he'd tossed it.

He hesitated for a fraction of a second and then he snatched it up, barely wanting to touch it at all, that nightmare still fresh in his mind, and he thrust it back down into its sheath.

Ready for when he needed it.

4

BREAKOUT

LOU BROUGHT his dark cloak around him, wrapping himself up so that only his eyes were exposed. He had to move quickly, and as silently as he could. Just as Hildie had been instructing him.

His friends' lives depended on it.

His heart throbbed in the pit of his throat, and he could feel the blood surging round his body as he bounded out over the plains, sticking to the few trees, to the night-time shadows where the Moon's milky-white light failed to reach.

He still felt parched, and he realised that he was sweating profusely, that the nightmare was still scarred into his mind, and he knew that his brain was telling him that he might have to kill again soon.

He paused beneath one of the trees in the middle of the plains to catch his breath. He pushed himself up against the tree trunk as hard as he could. Never in his life had he ever strived to take so much care, because now he knew that any hope that Sully and Rut had of being rescued rested on him keeping himself out of the hands of the Royal Guards.

He could feel the breeze coming down along the plains, flowing towards him from the direction of the approaching procession. He could smell the horse sweat on it, and, he was sure, the grease of the iron bars of the gaoler's cart.

He reached down to his waist and touched the handle of the Webbing Blade tentatively, just trying it out.

The chill almost burned his fingers.

He tore them back, almost lost himself and muttered a curse. But he retained control, and stared off into the moonlit plains, to the procession, growing closer by the second.

Heading right for him.

As Lou stood there, looming in the shadows, he felt his pulse quicken, and a strange sense of jubilation shred right through him.

He could already imagine the surprise, and then the joy, spread out on Sully and Rut's faces. He knew that if they'd bought into any of the stories about Onderswort that they'd have given up all hope. They knew that their lives from now on were to be merely half-lives, acted out as members of the living dead.

Lou breathed in more gently, trying to calm his quickening heart. He gripped hold of the handle of the Webbing Blade again, and he felt its influence chill him a little more.

He was almost certain that the Blade could tell when death lurked nearby.

He watched the horsemen draw closer.

Closer still.

A few minutes trot away, that was all they were.

He just needed to stay calm, and act quickly.

He had to use surprise.

That was all he had.

Lou kept his eyes fixed to the procession, and, just like Hildie had told him: when he found himself confronted with a large group of adversaries, he just needed to concentrate on one of them at a time.

But *seven* of them. There were *seven*.

The only way he could start was to pick out his first adversary.

Almost at once he got him in his sights.

A guard riding a little to the fringe of the procession, his horse several paces away from the rest. It would be the perfect diversion. The whole procession would stop. The men would form up, and Lou could then proceed to pick them off one by one.

All *seven* of them.

Before rescuing Rut and Sully.

The plan was so simple.

So, why was it so hard to get his feet to move?

Lou listened to the panting of the horses, and the smell of their sweat carried up his nostrils, tanged at the back of his mouth. He reached down to his side for the Webbing Blade, and shifted through the shadows, doing his best not to trip up on the uneven ground beneath his boots.

He kept his eyes fixed on the procession as he went, determined to keep them in his sights. He had to know just where they were so that he came at them from the right direction. If he made a small mistake, one tiny one, then it would not only be a case of them discovering him, but of his friends Sully and Rut being lost forever.

To Onderswort.

And so, with that on his mind, he crouched down below the line of the long grass and he waited, peering out from between the grass blades to the moonlight-flooded plains sweeping out before him.

To the procession of Royal Guards trotting their way in his direction.

His heart hammered against the back of his tongue, and his vision turned fuzzy from staring so hard, from wanting this so much. He was determined that he would be the one to save his friends, that he would rescue them from the horrors of Onderswort.

The hooves sounded on the earth now, he could feel the vibration as they dug up the earth and then tossed it off in their trail.

Lou gripped tight to the handle of the Webbing Blade, and felt its cool chill against his skin, almost freezing the bones of his hands solid . . . but not quite.

And he recognised the swirling power within himself, or at least he did now, ever since Hildie had *taught* him how to recognise it.

The horses plodded closer, their riders juddering a little in the saddle with each step. And soon Lou could hear the distinct *creak* of the wheels on the gaoler's cart. And he almost swore to himself that he could see his two friends nestled inside there.

Trapped beyond the bars.

Lou slid the Webbing Blade gently from its sheath, and he prowled through the grass, eyes still fixed on the horseman slightly apart from the rest, riding off on his own. Lou knew what he was. He knew enough about military strategy, from talk back in the fields, when he'd been a simple working hand, to know that this man's responsibility was that of a scout.

The man was supposed to scope out danger, and to alert the group of its presence.

Well, what happened when the danger spotted the scout first?

Lou guessed he was about to find out.

He stole ever closer, taking care to keep his body below the level of the long grass, so that he would be out of sight. Even if one of the horsemen did spot him, they might well disregard Lou as just a bare patch of earth or, at worst, a boar foraging in the long grasses of the plains in the middle of the night.

Still, it would be better if they didn't see him at all.

He shifted his way, feeling the slight rustle of the long grass against his trouser leg. Now was the time to try. He wouldn't get a better chance than this—a more important occasion to try this out.

It was another trick Hildie had taught him.

The art of disappearing.

Or of making those around you forget they'd seen you at all.

Lou hummed the incantation to himself, the one that Hildie had taught him. And he felt it vibrate in his throat, run through his nerves and his bones. He closed his eyes and concentrated on the centre of his solar plexus, again just as Hildie had shown him.

The feeling was strange.

Otherworldly, almost.

He felt almost like liquid now, or perhaps something thicker. Like honey. Yes, a little like honey. And he knew that the charm had worked its magic. That he would be invisible to those Royal Guards. Just as Hildie had made herself invisible when she'd appeared to him as the hobblesman. The same charm she'd cast over Lou when the guard had come looking for him back at her house in Ilsnare.

The Crystal City seemed so far away now.

Almost like it was another life.

Slowly, still not completely trusting his charm work, he rose from the long grass, and stood up to his full height. He peered out over the approaching procession, to the mounted Royal Guards, and to the scout, now only a dozen or so paces away from him.

He drew calm, gentle breaths, and concentrated on just what Hildie had told him to do. He was to think of himself as being at one with the wind. Not a husk blowing on the breeze. The wind *itself*.

He stared through the gloom, to the approaching scout, and he held his breath.

It was one thing to fool men with his invisibility, but quite another to fool a horse.

The mounted scout carried no torch with him. Again, Lou knew that this was to increase his visibility. Back at the gaoler's cart, he could see the flicker of the flames within the lanterns that hung off its side, swaying slightly with the movement.

That lantern shed an orange glow over their group.

But the scout, he was out here, in the darkness.

Cold and alone.

Lou wasn't sure whether he caught the horse's eye, or if the horse caught his eye first, but before he knew it, the horse flushed its nostrils and reared up on its hind legs.

He watched on as the mounted scout first tried to hold on, to scrabble his way up the horse's neck, before finally losing his balance and tumbling down into the long grass.

The horse whinnied and then galloped off in the direction it had come.

Headed back towards the gaoler's cart.

Lou hesitated, standing his ground. He felt his breath warming the air before his eyes, and a new stillness overcoming him. He heard the guards back in the procession calling out to the downed member of their group.

Lou stared at the grass, to where the scout had fallen, crumpling the long grass beneath him. And Lou wished that he would stay put. That he would see sense and just lay where he lay. Because if he was already dead, then Lou would have no need to kill him.

The scout poked his head up from where he lay in the long grass.

Lou gripped the handle of the Webbing Blade tighter still.

5

STALKING PREY

LOU FELT his whole body shudder with apprehension as he trudged through the long grass. The other members of the procession all called out. He noticed that one of the mounted Royal Guards had ridden off in the direction of the fleeing horse, gone off to catch it.

Well, at least that was one less guard that Lou would have to worry about for the time being.

Still, *seven* of them.

But one on the ground.

And the other chasing off across the plains.

Just four on horseback.

One driving the gaoler's cart.

He could do this.

Lou watched as the dismounted scout straightened up from the grass. When he turned to glance round himself, still blinking his eyes, obviously caught in a daze from his tumble, he stared right at Lou.

Or should that be, right *through* Lou?

Because one thing was for certain, Lou's invisibility charm worked just fine.

The scout waited another few seconds, and then a faint smile appeared on his lips. He called back to his companions, a jilt to his voice, a faint note of joviality. And, from the tone of the reply, the laughter back at the procession, Lou guessed that this, most likely, wasn't the first time on their journey that a horse had been spooked and thrown off its rider.

Too bad that this time it would be grave.

It would be no laughing matter.

Lou stalked on through the long grass, keeping his breathing quiet, and the Webbing Blade down at his side. He felt himself melt into the wind out here, and the rising chill inside him. It began at the very base of his ribcage and climbed its way up.

As if using his ribs like the rungs of a ladder.

And then the chilling sensation rested right in his heart.

He held the Webbing Blade tight and snuck up right behind the scout, who was now picking his way through the long grass, in the direction of the rest of the procession, which was advancing towards him now.

Before the scout took so much as another step, Lou grabbed the man from behind and held his arm around his throat.

Again, just as Hildie had taught him.

He held the Webbing Blade a few inches away from the man's neck, knowing that the man would be able to feel the chill of the steel.

The scout was so stunned by Lou's swift movements that he seemed struck dumb for several seconds. Lou tightened his grip on the man's throat, leaving just enough room for him to gasp out.

To call out to his companions.

To lead them right into Lou's trap.

When the scout found his voice, he guessed correctly. ". . . *Muh . . . Mage!*"

In a way, through all the adrenalin pumping through Lou's body, and the tension stinging his muscles, Lou almost took the remark as a compliment. Of course he wasn't a fully-fledged mage. Yet. But if he had his way he would be soon.

Hildie was an excellent teacher.

The advancing procession slowed and then came to a stop.

As one, the guards whipped their crossbows off their shoulders and held them tight in their grips, pointed in their direction.

If they decided to fire then they would certainly kill their friend.

As for the mage, though, Lou would see to it that he escaped unscathed.

Lou fixed his eyes on the gaoler's cart, on the two huddled-up figures pressed up against the bars, steeped in shadow as the lantern bounced against the wooden planks at the side of the cart.

He turned his attention back to his own prisoner.

The scout was staring down at Lou's arm, or to where he might've seen the grip, to Lou's *invisible* arm wrapped about his throat. Lou felt the scout swallow hard, and he took his opportunity to tighten his hold even more.

He looked to the others and waited.

The wind blew hard across the plains. It howled through the caverns up in the hills overlooking them, and then rustled down into the valley, blowing the grass all around.

Lou gripped the Webbing Blade even tighter, and he told

himself to be patient. Not to make any rash actions here. After all, he held all the cards.

One of the members of the group, one of the Royal Guards, called out across the plains, still holding his crossbow in his hands, fixed on Lou . . . or where he supposed Lou to be. "Invisible you may be, *mage*. But don't think you won't die with a bolt through the chest, just like a mortal."

Lou had no intention of testing out this theory. He gripped the scout tighter and held the flat of the Webbing Blade to the man's neck for a fraction of a second.

The scout let out an almighty howl.

Several of the horses flinched and tried to turn their noses away. But their riders held firm, and yanked them back around with their reins.

Lou could almost taste that freezing cold hanging in the air, emanating from the Webbing Blade, billowing up against his skin. And if it made an impact on Lou, with ice magic in his veins, then there was no telling what havoc it wreaked on the scout.

Lou might soon be about to discover, when he slipped the Blade into the man's supple skin, how great his resistance to magic really was.

If the man had some magical blood in his body it might prolong his death.

But that was all it could do for him now.

Lou waited. He knew that he had to get the rest of the procession into a receptive mood. Although he was unseen to them, and he had a hostage, it didn't mean that he had won yet.

At the back of his mind he was hoping there might be some way to get out of this situation without having to kill at all.

But that might just have been wishful thinking.

When the mounted guard spoke again, there was a slight

unease in his voice, and Lou knew that it was the effect of being out here, on the plains, in the moonlight, facing down to a mage who'd cast an invisibility charm over himself.

Lou supposed, if he'd been in the guard's boots, he might well have felt the same way.

"What is it you want, *mage*?"

Lou felt the scout trembling in his grip now, and he was sure that the man would try and escape at any moment. He would slip, like a snake, from his grasp, and then the man's companions would fire off their crossbows.

Fill Lou with crossbow bolts.

Or would they?

Lou studied the men mounted on their horses, studied their crossbows, and he tried to judge just what they might be planning. *That* surely was their plan. And if Lou was to be successful then he would need to counter it as soon as possible.

"First put down your weapons," Lou said, impressed with the booming quality of his voice.

Maybe he would make a mage of himself after all.

He watched on as the mounted guard who had spoken tilted his head back and spoke with the rest of the men. And then he saw them lower their crossbows. They stopped short of slinging them back over their shoulders. But it was a start.

A bargaining position at least.

The mounted guard at the front of the group looked between his horse's ears, both his hands still gripping his lowered crossbow.

The scout squirmed a little in Lou's grasp, and Lou tightened his hold on the man. For good measure he pressed the flat of the Webbing Blade against the man's skin once more.

The scout groaned long and hard, and then he was still.

Lou turned his attention back to the mounted guard, and said, "I want you to turn your prisoners free, to hand them over to me."

The mounted guard remained serious, a frown sketched on his lips, his face half-lit by the lanterns hanging off the gaoler's cart. He made no motion to glance back to his companions, and Lou knew instinctively that this man was the superior here.

Perhaps he even knew Herimyre personally.

The man who Lou had intended to kill.

But he hadn't killed him.

He'd killed the *king*.

"Impossible," the mounted guard said.

That was just the response that Lou had expected. What else could these men say? Weren't they Royal Guards, loyal to the king?

. . . Whoever that might be now.

And yet, Lou knew just what the best test of loyalty was.

He replaced the Webbing Blade in its sheath, and still with his other arm wrapped about the scout's throat, he reached inside his cloak, into his inner pocket, and felt for the purse nestled there.

As he withdrew it, he heard the coins jangle inside. He brought it forwards, before him, and then whispered into the scout's ear, hoarsely, "Take this."

Lou watched on as the scout, his hand trembling terribly, held out his palm flat. Lou dropped the purse and watched it burst from the invisibility charm, and materialise there in the man's hand.

The scout gawped at it for several seconds, apparently more struck by this well-stuffed purse than by the invisible mage that was keeping him in a chokehold.

Guards were like that.

Lou looked to the mounted guard, the leader of the group, to see that he was staring just as the scout was, at the purse that had landed in his hand. The mounted guard looked away from the purse, and back in Lou's direction. "If that's only grung in there, then you'd be better off slitting my man's throat and suffering the bolts of our crossbows."

Lou felt himself tremble. He felt less confident without the Webbing Blade in his hand. And so he reached down, again to his sheath, and slipped it out. He held it tight in his fist again, and he felt more normal.

When Lou spoke again, he was surprised that his voice almost had a lilt to it, as if he was constantly on the verge of chuckling. "Oh, believe me," Lou said, "that's not grung in there. That's pure silver, scavenged from the Sable Mountains."

He was sure that he saw the mounted guards' eyes widen, all of them simultaneously. And he felt the breath stick at the back of his throat, knowing that *soon* he would be reunited with his friends.

And all it had taken was that purse of silver.

That silver he'd collected from the villagers. The villagers had given it to him after a brief spout of resistance, and he'd had to remind them that Rut and Sully had kept them safe for years, that they'd served as skullers all over the plains, throughout all the villages, guarding them while they slept from the cursed animals that roamed the lands.

And so the least the villagers could do was buy their freedom.

The superior turned in his saddle, and looked back over his companions, all of them wearing tentative smiles now.

Lou saw that the guard who had galloped off to recover the scout's horse was returning now, that he held the escaped horse at the side of his own, walking their way back towards the procession. He supposed that they'd have a lot of explaining to do to him, to that guard.

But, Lou supposed, once the guard saw the purse full of silver it would go a long way to calming whatever reservations he might be having.

With the other mounted guards grinning all around him, the superior leaned forwards in his saddle, still clutching his crossbow tight, and he said, "First you show yourself to us, mage. And then we'll see about a deal."

6

A BARGAIN

LOU TURNED the proposal over in his mind. He stuck his
tongue into his cheek as he did so, a habit that he'd never
been able to shake ever since he'd been a schoolchild. He could
still feel the cold chill passing over his skin, and he could feel the
sensation kicking his heart into action.

The wind blew over the mounted guards all waiting before
him, and he caught another whiff of the scent of horses, that
mixture of manure and hot leather that seemed to be embossed in
his brain from ever since he'd been a child. Back in Endmere.
Listening to the horses trotting into the main square.

He watched their breath form clouds as the guards breathed,
as their horses breathed, and he squeezed the Webbing Blade
even tighter.

This whole scene just seemed so ghostly.

Almost unreal.

And, as he looked beyond the mounted guards, he now saw his
two friends, Sully and Rut, peering out between the bars. Their

withered faces staring at him. Their skin sallow in the lamplight, and their fingers, twisted like knotted tree roots, clung onto those iron bars.

Lou looked back to the superior, to the mounted guard still staring him down, and he said, "I'll only show myself if you dismount your horses, and lay down your weapons."

He waited, feeling his muscles shift slightly. He got a better grip of the scout's throat, felt the scout's spine pressed against his chest. The scout had a rigid, out-of-shape spinal cord, and he guessed that days and days of riding had done nothing to help its shape.

He looked over the guards, a new intensity in his eyes, although, he supposed, that it was a wasted effort.

After all, he was still invisible to them.

The superior smirked a little, his face almost folding into a monster's as he did so, but he made no reply. He simply glanced round, to the other five guards awaiting his orders, and then he stepped down from his horse.

The other guards did the same.

Lou allowed himself an exhale, and he started to have second thoughts about breaking his invisibility charm. Should he show himself so readily? He was a *mage*, after all, and as a class they certainly weren't renown for their honesty—for meeting promises.

No, they were known for being ruthless.

The *evil* ones anyway.

But Lou wasn't evil.

Lou wanted a few more moments to get himself together, to plot his plan of action, but the superior spoke before he could even think of where he might put his left foot.

"Come on, then, mage," the superior said. "Show yourself, and then show us that silver of yours." He looked back to his men, and then, as one, they each dropped their crossbows into the long grass before them. He looked to Lou and said, "Now it's your turn."

But Lou wasn't so easily tricked. He still saw the swords at their waists, the daggers slipped into their belts. Which was to say nothing for whatever hidden weapons they were each surely carrying.

One could never be too careful when venturing out onto the plains.

Lou demanded they drop the rest of their armoury, and, with the superior sighing hard, and his shoulders rising and then falling rapidly, they did so.

"Is that enough?" the superior said. "Or won't you be satisfied until you've got us all down to our underwear?"

One of the guards, behind the superior, let loose a nervous laugh.

The superior, grim-faced, glanced round, and the laughter stopped.

Lou felt the wind stirring again, whipping its way through the tall grass once more, blowing his cloak up against his body. He *was* the wind. He was *one* with the wind. Could he really let this go so easily? Could he voluntarily drop his invisibility charm?

He would've been the first to admit that, during his training sessions with Hildie, he'd had many issues with coming back from the charm, breaking out of it.

Making himself visible.

And yet he would have to do so now, if he was to keep his promise.

If he *wanted* to keep his promise.

Lou pressed his lips tight together, and he squeezed the handle of the Webbing Blade all the more. He still held the scout in his chokehold, and even if he made himself visible he had no intention whatsoever of letting the man go.

Not until he'd watched the rest of the soldiers slip over the horizon.

Not until he was quite sure they wouldn't be coming back.

Lou sucked up the fresh, night air and felt it fill up his lungs. He felt better, more at peace with nature, almost at home out here on the plains. And these men, their horses, their stinks and their noise, that was the real pollutant here.

And yet, for now, in the situation Lou found himself in, he knew that he had to play by their rules.

Or at least appear to.

So, with his heart throbbing its way up his throat, and his blood thickening—or was it freezing?—he squeezed his eyes shut once again and he muttered the now-familiar incantations.

The ones he'd practised over and over with Hildie.

And he felt himself tingle all over.

Even though Lou had his eyes shut, he knew that he had returned to the world of the visible. He heard the horses snort, the stirring of hooves, and—he was almost certain of it—the stench of horse manure being rapidly expelled.

He felt their eyes on him.

He waited another few heartbeats, and then he opened his eyes.

Just as he'd imagined it, they were all staring at him. And as the realisation dawned on him, he almost let his fingers slip from the throat of scout.

Thankfully, the scout didn't seem to notice.

The superior of the guards smirked at him. "Thought you might be a bit bigger than that." He nodded to the scout, who Lou still clung on tight to. "Though Parc never was one of the strongest in the Royal Guards."

As if in response to his superior's cutting criticism, the scout —*Parc*, apparently—went a little limp in Lou's grip. Still, despite the superior's claim, there was no way Lou was going to give Parc any more slack to play with.

If he let go of Parc now, Lou would be a dead man.

Even with the guards' weapons lying in the long grass before them.

He guessed that they were well drilled at picking up weapons with speed, and they could probably leap back up onto their horses' backs just as quick.

No, Lou had to take extreme care now.

The superior nodded in his direction. "So, *mage*. Now that we can see you, how are we going to do this? It seems like you're holding all the cards."

But, over the superior's head, some movement caught Lou's eye.

He couldn't be certain, but, in the moonlight, he saw the leaves stirring at the top of a large tree. Probably the largest tree on the plains, thinking about it. And he kept his focus up there. Kept on staring. But he just couldn't see it again.

"Hello?" the superior said, with a mocking tone. "Got somewhere to be?" he said, and then turned round and looked to where Lou was staring. "Someone back there, is there? Got a companion with you?"

For another few moments, Lou just kept staring on, back to the spot at the top of the tree. And, the more he thought about it, the surer he was about what he'd seen.

A crow.

No, *the* crow.

The one from his dream.

He regained his senses just in time to see the superior cast a glance back over his men, no doubt planning some sort of a sneak attack. But, Lou was glad to see, all their weapons seemed to be very much still bundled in the long grass, at their feet.

Lou turned his mind to the practicalities of the bargain, and then said, "All right, how's this, how about we walk over to you —*real* slow—and then you all back away from the cart, you know so that you're a little way away from those weapons of yours."

The superior smirked again. "You must be joking," he said. "You think we're gonna walk right into your little friend's, or *friends*', trap, then you've got another thing coming entirely. You think we were born yesterday?"

Lou considered his options. He wasn't really in the position to make threats, not unless he wanted to find himself caught up in a pitched battle. If any of them got hold of their weapons they'd kill him. There would be no doubt about it.

No, he needed to compromise.

If he was going to save Sully and Rut, that was.

"Okay," Lou said, hearing the breeze blow through the leaves on the trees.

The Moon slipped behind a cloud, a cloud that Lou hadn't previously noted. And he wouldn't have noted that if he hadn't earlier noted that it was a particularly clear night tonight. No clouds in sight.

In any case, the plains slipped into that dim, post-midnight light, and he felt a shudder crawl up his arm from the handle of the Webbing Blade. The only real light out here now, the only thing standing between them and the night, was the shaggy lantern light from the gaoler's cart.

Lou shuffled forwards, kicking the heels of the scout's boots to get him walking.

But not too fast.

Lou made sure to keep the Webbing Blade only a hair's breadth away from the scout's neck, and he made sure to keep as much of his body as he could hidden behind the scout, so that if he noticed any of the guards rush for their weapons then he'd have half a chance of using his hostage as a human shield.

But that would still leave six of them.

Six against one.

And Sully and Rut watching on from behind the bars, there to witness his demise.

Lou stepped closer and closer, keeping his eyes watchful, over the whole of the group of guards, trying his best to keep them all in his vision, so that he'd see them so much as twitching a muscle.

The stink of the horses was almost unbearable now, and he caught a whiff of that leathery smell, of the sheaths the guards carried, that taste that always seemed to stick way at the back of his throat.

He listened to the slightly damp earth suck at the soles of his boots, and he tried to slow his heartbeat, tried to play his part.

He had to show them Louson Dorf the Fearsome Ice Mage.

Not Lou the Timid Working Hand.

And so he locked eyes with the superior guard.

He stared into those purple-brown eyes of his, the colour of his irises made all the more odd, otherworldly, by the lantern light from the gaoler's cart. And he saw the firmness of the man's cheekbones, and he had no need to take in the rest of the man's body, no need to lower his gaze to the man's torso, to know that he was a well-built, muscular man.

Certainly more than capable of beating Lou to death unarmed.

Even if Lou had the Webbing Blade in his hand, like he did now.

They drew closer, making their steady progress, over to the procession. And Lou could see the slight glint of the sword blades, still lying in the grass, from the lantern that hung from the gaoler's cart. He dared not sneak a look at the gaoler's cart itself, to Rut and Sully, surely both of them standing up there, staring out at him with wild hope.

At the back of his mind, Lou had almost convinced himself that none of this was real.

When they got within half a dozen paces or so, the superior clicked his fingers.

It took Lou a couple of moments to realise that he was indicating the purse that the scout still held in his hand. Lou had almost forgotten about the purse. Almost forgotten about just how he was going to bargain for Sully and Rut's lives.

Lou brought the scout to a halt with a jerk, feeling his grip tighten around the man's neck, and he squeezed the Webbing Blade a little more.

He felt the chill scour his heart.

The superior looked to Lou, a grin now stretched across his lips. "Listen here, *mage*, let's not have any bad blood here, right? You know how it is. Sure, we serve the king, but we've all got families, we're working men, see?" His grin dulled a little, but the sparkle never left those purple-brown eyes. "Not that a mage would know much about a hard day's work, though."

Lou knew far more about a hard day's work . . . a whole bunch of summers' hard work for that matter . . . but this hardly seemed the moment to pick bones with the superior, and especially considering that Lou was acting the part, that as far as these guards knew, he *was* a fearsome mage.

Let them believe whatever they liked.

The superior held up his hands, and the guards behind him did the same, to show that none of them had weapons and, furthermore, that none of them would make a grab for the weapons before them, nestled in the grass, while the exchange took place.

Lou held his breath, and sucked in his cheeks, made his face look more gaunt, hoped to make himself look a little more threatening.

The superior started towards him. As he walked, there was a *jingle* from his belt, a *jingle* that Lou realised was most likely to be the keys to the gaoler's cart. Lou kept his focus on the man's eyes, not wanting to get distracted.

He'd almost done it now.

Soon Sully and Rut would be free.

Next up, Lou could smell that oniony breath that all working men seemed to have—he'd had it once upon a time, when he'd boiled up a broth for breakfast on his way out to the fields. He could still taste that greasy warmth on his tongue.

Sometimes Lou even dreamed about its taste, dreamed back to the old days.

When he didn't dream about killing the king, that was.

The superior guard continued on his way, just a couple of paces away now.

All of a sudden it seemed like Lou had a hundred places to look, that it took all his concentration to keep an eye on the guards over the superior's shoulders. He did his best to keep a tight hold of the scout. That was his one bargaining chip in this exchange, and if he let it go he was done for.

More than done for.

He was *dead*.

The superior took the final step, exhaled a long, wafting lungful of broth into the chilly night air, and then he reached forwards, and took the purse from the scout's hand.

First he weighed the purse in his hand, and Lou heard it jangle a little, listened to the silver pieces all jostling against one another. Then he wrapped the drawstring around his chubby index finger and Lou saw the finger was covered with lacerations from all the crossbow shooting ... or so he guessed.

The superior undid the string and then tipped the contents of the purse out onto his palm.

The coins all jostled out of the bag, and they reflected the lantern light from the gaoler's cart. Lou was aware that the other guards were trying to steal a glance, standing on their tiptoes, trying to get a look around the body of their superior, to see whether this was real.

The superior guard took one of the silver pieces between thumb and forefinger, held it up to the dull lantern light, and then he stuck it between his lips and bit into it.

Lou waited with apprehension. He felt his lungs prickle, and sweat dampen the back of his tunic, beneath his cloak. All of a sudden all the freshness had gone from the air, and everything seemed stale.

Just the stench of the horses, the stink of the superior's breath, the body odour of the scout that he still held onto tight.

Lou's stomach churned, but he kept a hold on himself. He had to stay strong now. He had to show them that he wasn't afraid.

The superior brought the silver coin back out of his mouth,

glanced over it again, and then nodded to himself. He slapped it down with the rest of the silver coins and then tipped them back into the velvet-clothed purse. He drew the drawstring tight and then slipped it into the front pocket of his tunic.

When he turned his gaze to Lou, Lou saw the half-smile, curling back one corner of his mouth, and maybe he should've taken it as a warning. But he'd been so sure that he'd won. That soon he would spring Sully and Rut free.

But then the superior said, "Duck!" and the scout just slipped from Lou's grasp, slithered away from him, and the fist flew into the ridge of Lou's nose.

And then everything went black.

And a colossal ringing seemed to try and wrench his skull apart.

7

TRICKED

LOU COULDN'T get a hold of his surroundings several seconds. He wasn't even sure if he was awake or sleeping.

Or knocked out.

He felt his brain prickle, and all the muscles in his body draw taut, and his heart pound hard in his chest, as if threatening to break through his ribs.

And then the stench of piss caught him, and he rolled over onto his side and puked over the floor.

The floor.

That was right.

He stretched his palm out and felt along the ridged wood, the rotten, and splintered wood. And then he heard the *creak* of the wagon wheels, and the plodding of horses' hooves.

And he knew just where he was.

Inside the gaoler's cart.

The numbness clawed over his skin, and he could taste the blood in his mouth. When he reached up to touch his nose, it felt out of place, twisted off to the side. And after only a moment or two of touching it, impossible, overwhelming pain struck him.

"Ahh!" he said, only realising that he'd muttered that groan a few seconds after it lingered out in the air before him.

The blood on his upper lip was dried. But there was a ton of it. He seemed to have more blood than skin there right now.

And then, as he padded his body for more damage, an even worse realisation dawned on him.

He didn't have the Webbing Blade.

"Lou?"

The voice was gasping, as if it came from a hollow chest. And when Lou looked up, strained his eyes to peel back the gloom, to see into the darkened corners of the gaoler's cart, he saw that the chest might well be hollow after all. What he could have no doubts about, however, was just who the voice came from.

Rut.

Even here, in this gloomy, dingy, moving gaol cell, Lou could see his blond hair, and he was almost certain he could see the twinkle of moonlight in those blue eyes of his. His body, though, it was nothing like he remembered.

The rolling gut was gone.

In fact, Rut looked skeletal, and much smaller.

Before Lou could think to respond to Rut, he was already turning his attention to the other corner of the gaoler's cart, to where he saw the other form, the other beaten-up body.

Sully.

Unlike Rut, Sully apparently couldn't so much as find the strength to raise his voice, to speak to his would-be rescuer.

Even despite the situation, despite this impossibly bad situation that Lou now found himself in—clearly heading to Shildersmoore, and then to be put on a ship, to arrive in Onderswort and live out the rest of his days in pain and darkness, and mud—Lou let loose a hysterical giggle.

Some rescuer he'd turned out to be!

Lou felt his heart leaping about inside his chest, and the sweat still sticking to his tunic and causing him to shiver from the breeze that blew in through the bars of the gaoler's cart.

He was doomed!

They were *all* doomed now!

"Lou?" Rut said, again. "Are you ... are you okay?"

Lou felt a tingle spark through his body, dance about his nerves, and all of a sudden the mood inside of him seemed to grow more sombre. And now it seemed a totally inappropriate moment for him to laugh.

This was no time for laughing.

This was a time for sobbing.

But he just didn't have the strength.

"They chained us up," Rut said. "After they knocked you out and shoved you in here." He gave a slight *jangle* of his chains, as if to prove his point.

And only then did Lou realise that he was free. He *didn't* have chains. He moved his arms and legs all about, as if to prove this. But that didn't matter. Now that he didn't have the Webbing Blade they were all defeated.

Unless he could find a way to get his hands back on it, he might as well just give up and die here now, spread himself out and *die* on the floor.

"How did you find us?" Rut said.

Lou slumped up against the bars of the cart, and felt the throb and jerk of the cart jangling his bones. He seemed to feel every hop of the road, every misstep of one of the horses. And he could almost imagine himself feeling each and every stinging lash of the reins coming down on those horses' backs.

"A hobblesman," Lou said.

Rut remained quiet for a few seconds, and then he said, "Yeah, that's right! I remember the man, when we stopped. Spent quite a while looking into the cart. Didn't speak to either of us, though. Wanted to know where we were going. And after he sold the guards something they seemed just happy to tell him whatever it was he wanted to know."

Lou felt his head spin now. He knew that the hobblesman no longer mattered, all that mattered was where they were headed.

Onderswort.

That was their destination.

Their final destination.

"Thanks for trying," Rut said. "I mean . . . I mean, being back in the gaols, back in Ilsnare, we thought you'd forgotten us. Silly really. But that was what we thought. You got to somewhere safe, you got the rest of the villagers to somewhere safe?"

Lou nodded, and then, realising that most likely Rut couldn't make out subtle movements in the gloom, he managed a limp, and defeated, "Yeah," and then, trying a little harder, "they're safe."

"Good, good," Rut said, jangling his chains a little as he said it. "I mean, that's *great*, really it is, that's the most important thing. That you've got them somewhere safe, that they don't need to *suffer* any longer, right?"

"I suppose," Lou said, and then he turned his attention to the other corner of the cart, to where he could just about make out the form of Sully hanging, from his own set of chains. "What about you, eh, Sully?" Lou said. "Haven't heard a peep out of you yet." He felt that same giddy, hysterical rush bounce through him, and he had no chance of cutting it from his tone. "Not gone all *crazy* in the gaols, have you?"

"Lou," Rut said, this time with a slightly muffled voice, as if he might be afraid of waking a sleeping infant. "Thing is, with Sully, you know, he's been all quiet now for a long time. Well, you know that he was never the most talkative, but one day, in the gaols, he just shut up, and he's been like that ever since."

Lou stared into the gloom of the cart, tried to make out more of Sully, perhaps he was trying to catch his eye, to see something that would strike him as familiar. But the darkness was thick and almost impenetrable.

With nothing else left to do, Lou decided to rest his eyes. He slumped over on the floor of the cart and felt his nose throbbing, as if threatening to pop off his face at any moment of its choosing. He didn't care any more. He just didn't care.

Without the Webbing Blade he was nothing.

He was just Lou the Working Hand.

Certainly not Louson Dorf the Ice Mage.

As the sun rose up over the horizon, brushed at the tops of the trees, and the birdsong started, Lou felt the cart slowing down. And he heard the *squelch* of mud winding its way around the wagon wheels. He could smell it on the air. Thickening the air.

He listened as the guards' horses plodded all round them

Now this was certainly a pitched battle.

It would be three men, two of them half-starved, against seven fully-armed and healthy Royal Guards. Oh, and the *three* of them were locked up to start with.

Two of them in chains.

No chance.

As the daylight leaked into the gaoler's cart, Lou began to make out Sully's appearance, he started to be able to make out his face, to see those familiar features of his.

He still had his wiry frame, of course he did, the neck-long, jet-black hair too . . . and the matching eyes. Those eyes, Lou really had no idea what he'd expected of them. Had he expected to see him sleeping, those eyelids clamped shut?

Well, what he got was Sully staring out, into mid-air, into the centre of the gaoler's cart, into something that neither Lou or Rut could see.

Lou tried to speak to him, but gave up shortly after. He understood almost right away what Rut had said, that Sully had just stopped speaking. He had stopped *seeing* too, and most likely hearing, tasting, touching or smelling as well.

If the despair that Lou felt right now, for their situation, their *utterly* dreadful situation, was even a fraction of what Sully was feeling, then he could understand him. In fact, Lou wondered how Rut had managed to hold out for so long—how he'd kept himself relatively sane in the face of what was to be . . . for want of a better word . . . a living *hell*.

Still, Lou managed to scratch those doom-laden thoughts from the forefront of his mind, and he decided to bring Rut up to speed on things. To tell him about just what he'd missed.

When he told Rut about the silver, that he'd got it from the villagers, that they'd all pitched in to help spring them free, Rut got all quiet again.

Almost as deathly silent as Sully.

The wagon trundled onwards, and the mud still squelched its way through the wheels. He could hear the horses puffing hard as they pressed on, did their best to push their way across the uneven terrain.

Lou looked out the back of the gaoler's wagon, to the way they'd come. He worked his gaze up from the deep trench-like marks the cartwheels had left behind in their path, those ridges of mud parted like a well-ploughed field, and then to the endless plains stretching out behind them.

And then further up.

The sky had clouded over, and the whole landscape stretched out behind them was grey. He was sure that it was fog hanging down over the land. He could smell the rain hanging in the air, as if ready to fall at any moment.

Although he'd never been to the coast, he'd always supposed that it was something like this. Could he smell a slight scent of salt in the air, crisp on the thickening breeze? Or was it just his imagination, that suggestion of salt just making his mouth water?

Soon they would be at Shildersmoore, the port.

At first, Lou couldn't place the sound. He thought it was the breeze in the trees, blowing the leaves around, or perhaps the sound of a field of long grass, all its blades rustling against one another. But then, as he propped himself up, straightened his back, and peered out through the gap in the iron bars, he saw what it really was.

Crows.

Hundreds of them.

No, more like thousands.

Hundreds of thousands.

8

A FLOCK OF CROWS

LOU FELT HIS CHEST TIGHTEN, and his mind stretch back to that time when, out on the hill, well away from the pit-black walls of Ilsnare, he'd been training with Hildie. It was back when he'd still believed that she was a hobblesman, when she'd *deceived* him.

His heart throbbed in his throat, and he could feel a thin layer of sweat seep out of his skin, and the light breeze blow up against him, and carry away any remaining heat he might've had in his blood.

The crows, the flock of crows, it was so thick that it blocked out the sun. He stared up at it, almost convinced that it was a delusion. He thought back to the crow from his dream, the one which sat on the branch outside the king's quarters, just as he prepared to throw himself off the ledge. But this wasn't just one crow. There were far too many to count.

And they were flapping their way towards them, seemingly pursuing the gaoler's cart, no, descending on it.

He listened to the hundreds of thousands of pairs of flapping wings, and he was almost certain he could smell that muddy scent that he'd always associated with bird feathers. And he felt raw, unchecked fear flood through him.

He hadn't seen cursed animals for ages, not for seasons now, and he'd almost come to believe that they were some untouchable aspect of his past that he could afford to forget.

Now, though, he knew that the cursed animals, the animals which came from Ilsnare, The Crystal City, were just as real as they'd always been.

It didn't matter that they'd been out of sight for a while.

Lou scrabbled to his feet, a task made more difficult by the moving cart, constantly jerking its way over the muddy track. He found his way over to Rut, lying propped up, still in chains, and snoring away, his mouth latched open and a droplet of spittle accumulating at the corner of his lips.

"Rut!" Lou said. "Rut!"

Rut shuddered long and hard, and then he screwed up his features, turned his head away. And it took Lou a moment to realise that Rut was waiting for him to strike him.

Lou guessed that was the treatment Rut had had to get used to back in the gaol in Ilsnare.

Soon enough, though, when Rut found that the strike wasn't forthcoming, he cracked open his eyes and then opened them fully, seeming to realise just where he was. That they were all still here in the gaoler's cart, and that Lou was there with him.

"Look!" Lou said, jabbing his finger to indicate the flock of crows, all bustling together, their *ca-kaws!* splitting the thick and foggy air hanging down over the plains.

Rut turned slowly, only really able to move his head, as his arms and legs were bound with the clanking chains. As he looked, his eyes widened and his mouth latched even further open than when he'd been sleeping.

Before he had the chance to say anything, Lou heard one of the mounted guards, outside the gaoler's cart, call out to the others.

And the cart rocked to a halt.

Lou kept his balance, gripping tight to the iron bars, feeling the iron press against the palm of his hand, and he kept as still as he could, watching as the guards, still mounted on their horses, rushed past the cart, crossbows in their hands, and began to let fly at the sky.

At the flock of crows bearing down on the procession.

Lou watched the bolts whistle through the air, all of them finding a target. He watched the crow bodies drop out of the sky and land with those sickening, almost moist *thuds* in the long grass. But the shots made no effect on the crows' numbers, or their resolve.

They just kept coming.

Lou felt almost paralysed, standing up there, his nose between the bars of the gaoler's cart as he watched the guards swarm into a V-shaped formation, and begin to concentrate their fire. He counted six of them there.

All of them except for the driver, obviously still upfront, perhaps still gripping the reins in his hands, balancing the option of fleeing the scene, of abandoning his friends, with the sanctity of safety.

Lou didn't need to have had a previous experience with cursed crows, like he'd had with Hildie, to know that these men had no chance of mounting a resistance against the oncoming flock of crows.

What they needed now was a mage.

But they kept up their crossbow fire, their bolts still fizzling through the air, and the soot-coloured, little bodies continued to drop from the sky.

Lou beat himself out of his daze, of watching that approaching, enormous black cloud of crows bearing down on them, and he turned his attention back to the interior of the gaoler's cart, to Sully hunched up in the corner, still bound in chains, and still staring into mid-air, the air before him. Apparently totally indifferent to these cursed crows.

Lou knew that they weren't safe. Not even here locked away in the cart. He knew that the crows would slither in between the bars, and they'd come to peck out their eyeballs, to gorge on their tongues, and, with them still alive, begin to stab away at their abdomens, for the richest treats of all.

And he knew that if they . . . if *any* of them . . . were to escape from this situation, then he would need to be free.

And he would need to have the Webbing Blade in his hand.

Lou wasted no time. The fluttering of the wings, and the frequency of the *ca-kaws* rattled the air, almost seemed to make it throb, absorbing all other sounds. Absorbing the wind itself.

Lou called out to the superior among them, the man who sat on the back of his horse, in the pit of the V-shape, and who seemed to be firing off twice as many crossbow bolts as the rest of the guards.

Lou cupped his hands around his mouth, trying to get the man to hear him, but either he ignored him, or he simply couldn't hear him over the crows' calls and the beating of wings.

He kept on screaming out, till his lungs burned right to the base of his ribcage, and he felt the blood begin to swell in his temples, and almost overwhelm his brain.

The superior guard finally turned in his saddle, a sneer fixed on his lips, and a matted quality to his eyes. When he shouted back to Lou, he had no problem whatsoever in understanding him. "What's the matter, mage? Afraid to die? If we're to die, then we shall die together."

With that, the superior turned back to the approaching crows, and continued to let his bolts fly.

Lou turned his attention back to the inside of the gaoler's cart and tried to make himself think, to imagine some way that they might be able to get themselves out of this place.

His wondering was answered when he heard the soggy *squelch* of boot steps at the side of the cart.

He glanced round, looked through the bars, to where he saw the driver.

The man was easily the oldest of the guards, perhaps fifty or more, and, as Lou could deduce, he wasn't trusted with much more than the driving itself. He carried his crossbow down at his thigh, pointed to his toes, and his eyes slipped about their sockets as he absorbed the sheer hopelessness of the situation.

Lou had learned a lot about bartering with people from Hildie, and Rule One of her book was always to have money to offer. Well, that was the strategy he'd put into practice back before he'd got himself knocked out and captured. All told it had been quite effective, not withstanding that he'd been a touch sloppy with the details.

He didn't have money to offer now.

But, in a way, he had something much more valuable to offer.

Survival.

9

A GLIMMER OF HOPE

LOU RUSHED OVER, across the floor of the cart, hearing the wooden floorboards creak loudly beneath his boots, and he confronted the man—the driver—who continued to stare blankly up to the sky, up to where the crows lingered over them.

"My knife!" Lou cried out, over the caterwaul of the fluttering wings and bird cries. "Get me my knife if you want to live!"

The driver, apparently still struck with shock, slowly turned his head to look at Lou. And Lou could almost swear that he observed the cold sweat dampen the man's face. The man made no response. Nor did he move either of his feet.

"Listen to me!" Lou said. "If you want to live go and get my dagger! Get it now!"

Just then, Lou heard the first scream come from one of the guards. He spun round and saw the flock of crows had descended to be right overhead, and that the first crows were attacking, their talons opened wide and ready to catch any slab of supple human skin they could.

One of the guards had a pair of crows with their talons dug into his scalp, and the two of them were pecking away at his head. He was beating at them with both his hands. And Lou watched on as the horse he rode first pricked its ears and then let loose a huge whinny, and reared up.

The man slipped off the saddle and plummeted to the ground. He continued to scrabble with his hands, still screaming out. His legs thrashed too, but it only seemed to incense the crows, and they just pecked harder.

And more soon came to join them, as if sensing the blood ready to spill.

Lou could see the pin-prick red eyes, and that just confirmed what he already know. That these crows were cursed. That they were part of the curse which Hildie's father, Ma'reygar, had cast over Ilsnare years ago.

And they'd come all the way out here, out to the very edge of the Kingdom of Shellacnass, to feast on them.

The driver continued to stand there gawping.

Lou's eyes fell down to the man's waist, searching for something, *anything*, that might help them out there. But the man only had his whip hanging from his belt, and a dagger.

Not the Webbing Blade.

A lot of good a *normal* dagger would do them all now.

If only Lou had known how to pick a lock, then he might've been able to do something for them. And that gave him an idea.

He thrust his arm through the bars and caught hold of the sleeve of the driver's tunic.

The driver was so taken aback that he lost his footing, slipped up in the mud, and fell against the side of the cart, bumping his head.

Thankfully, though, he didn't knock himself out. He stayed

conscious. If he blacked out on them now then that would be the end of all of their hopes.

"The keys!" Lou said, shouting so loud that it made his ears ring. "You've gotta let us out of here."

The driver met Lou's eye, and his lower lip trembled. And then he shook his head, over and over again, before glancing off in the direction of the other guards, to those still firing off at the crows.

The other guards were becoming overwhelmed now, each of them having to contend at close quarters with the crows pecking at them, snagging their talons in their tunics.

The guard who had fallen to the ground now made no sound. His limbs had gone still apart from the odd twitch of a finger or the kick of the foot.

Lou felt a tingle run through his chest and he resolved that that wasn't going to happen to them, *none* of them. He hadn't come out here, come to rescue Rut and Sully, only to die at their sides. He would save them. He would save them all.

And then, Lou realised, following the driver's gaze, that the superior guard had the ring of keys at his belt, that he had the Webbing Blade, snug in its sheath there too.

He looked back at the driver just in time to see a dozen or more crows flutter over him, land on his head, and flatten him to the ground, screaming out and scrabbling with his arms to no effect.

A couple of heartbeats later and there was no sound.

And Lou knew that the driver was dead.

Lou stared as the crows moved in, as their feathered bodies descended on the driver, covering him completely. And he heard the chewing, the ripping of flesh, and, over everything else, the squabbling *ca-kaw!* calls over and over again.

He descended back into the cart and looked to Sully and Rut, knowing that, right now, it seemed like they were truly going to die. That this was the end now. And he might as well make peace with that.

He turned to watch the guards' enduring struggle with the cursed crows, he watched as each of them, in turn, were smothered by the crows, and as that same gut-wrenching ripping of skin, and the pecking of bone, and the life-ending screams rocked the landscape.

For a few seconds, Lou could only hear his own heartbeat, and the gentle chill in his veins. That chill that he knew was his ice magic.

There was one thing that he could try.

But he'd only worked on it for a matter of minutes with Hildie.

Right before she'd left.

And he'd completely failed to make it work. It had been funny, almost, at the time, he remembered now laughing about it, shaking his head at his incompetence. Getting struck with that same feeling in his mind, the one that he would never *ever* make a real mage. That he was just a pretender.

Now, though, he had to try. There was no other option.

He turned his attention back to guards, to their battle with the crows, and their crossbow bolts still scattering, apparently aimless, into the blackening sky.

There was only one of them visible now, from within the cloud of crows, and that was the superior.

He had his dagger drawn now, and he was thrashing at any of the crows that came close to him, and hitting most of them. Lou watched as a crow would land on him, jab its needle-sharp talons into his shoulders, or his arm, or his thigh, and how the superior would swipe the bird out of the way, cut right through it.

But there were just too many.

And while the superior continued to fight his personal losing battle, the other guards, all around him, Lou could only identify from the black birds which smothered their corpses—or soon to be corpses—almost completely.

All he could see now was the sway of the crows' bulk as they fought to chew away at the best of the morsels, to get the juiciest pieces of the guards that they could manage.

And, even though the guard had tricked him, even though he'd thwarted his attempts to save his friends from their unjust fate, Lou felt something inside him as he watched the crows all land on top of the superior and, finally, with the force of their bulk, drive him to the ground, and down amongst his equally smothered companions.

The dark cloud continued to descend, and Lou knew that this feast was a long way from over. He knew that the crows hadn't forgotten about them, that they merely hadn't yet exhausted their stock of food outside the cart.

Would this be their fate?

Would they be forced to watch their captors consumed before the crows turned their insatiable hunger onto them, the prisoners?

Just as he watched the last scrap of the superior's tunic disappear between the thickly-packed bodies of crows, he lowered his head and began to mumble the charm.

Lou could feel the words humming in his throat. They never made their way out between his lips. They just seemed to throb in his mouth and dissolve. This had to work. And it had to work now. Else they were finished. They would end up as pecked-out corpses, just like the guards.

Just as he remembered when he'd tried this with Hildie, he could feel his blood throbbing in his veins, feeling like it was thickening, rolling its way into his chest, concentrating his power.

That was what Hildie had told him to do.

To imagine that his solar plexus, that it was like the centre of his soul.

And that everything shined out from his soul.

Lou pressed his eyes shut so tight that they stung. He clasped his fists hard, and felt his fingernails dig into his palms. And he was sure that he could feel the slick warmth of blood against his fingertips.

He crunched his teeth tight together, and tasted the enamel, was sure that he could feel his teeth splitting at the root. And he concentrated more than anything on his solar plexus, on focussing all his power, all the power within him, right there.

Several times he felt the charm ebbing away from him, and whenever he did, he did just as Hildie had instructed him. He spoke the words harder, with more feeling, and he allowed the charm to float inside of him, and then out of him, never grabbing for it.

And then he let it go.

10

A DEVASTATING BRIGHTNESS

I T WAS LIKE a rush of sparks, all tickling his chest. The sparks worked their way up his body, to his chin, and tickled him there too. And he felt his solar plexus relax, all his muscles around that spot where he was focussing just seem to lose their tightness.

At first the chill was devastating. So strong, and so surprising that he didn't even think to shudder. He just froze, remained locked in those few seconds for a long while. Although he had no presence of mind to open his eyes, he knew that if he'd tried then he would've found his eyelashes stuck solid.

Iced over.

Slowly, though, the world bounded back to him, in slick little leaps. Details bounced back to him. That warm stench of urine in the gaoler's cart, that musky scent of the crows' feathers, the feathers that he seemed to have breathed into his mouth, and now lay on his tongue.

And then, off in the very distance, he heard a sound not unlike the scraping of one sword blade on another, and its echo held and rung out in the air. Clamped itself on his hearing, drowning out everything else.

And that scraping remained suspended in the air, almost like a *hum* the scrape was so shrill, and only then did Lou think to open his eyes.

Lou's heart juddered up to his throat as he anticipated the sight before him. He cranked his eyelids open, one by one, and stared out all around him.

Close to him, inside the gaoler's cart, he could see Sully and Rut, both of them turned to look at him, Rut with his mouth agape, and eyes wild, while Sully looked to Lou with a matted expression.

That same death looking out from beneath the glassy veneer of his eyes.

They were all stuck in time, halted in motion as Lou's heart ticked on. He glanced up and around them. He took in the heavenly, iridescent orb that encapsulated them, that gleamed just like the bubbles on a soaped-up pail of water.

And he watched, slowly at first, almost *impossibly* slowly, as the crows pounded against the periphery of the bubble, and then, without exception, cracked their beaks, and snapped their necks, before plummeting to the ground on the outside of the bubble.

He had done it.

He had cast the protective charm.

He had saved them.

Lou bided his time, waiting there, feeling his shallow-lunged breaths lifting the front of his tunic. He looked about him, felt himself coming back to his senses, and time resuming its trot within the bubble.

When he spoke to Sully and Rut his voice was otherworldly, floating away from him as if it was far too light for the air to carry. "Are you okay?"

Rut continued to ogle Lou, but just about managed a nod.

Sully, on the other hand, continued to gape into mid-air, apparently untouched by just what had gone on. But he had been saved by it all the same.

Of course Rut was surprised, why wouldn't he be? He had no idea of the journey that Lou had been on, that he'd discovered that he had ice magic in his veins. Surely he'd witnessed Lou's display, his face off with the guard when he'd attempted to bargain for their lives, and he'd seen Lou had made himself invisible.

But, Lou supposed, examining things from Rut's perspective: his food, water and sleep-deprived state, he might just as well have believed it to be a mirage.

A simple parlour trick.

Perhaps he'd thought Lou had been playing a role, attempting to trick the guards by playing to their sensibilities, their fear of magic. And who wouldn't have been taken in, out here on the plains, a long way from the rhyme and reason of Ilsnare?

But now, seeing the protective charm that Lou had just cast, he knew that Rut could have no doubt that Lou could easily back up his claims of magic. That Lou was in fact a mage.

Or at least on the highroad to becoming one.

Lou felt himself fold up inside, and he reminded himself that he couldn't allow himself to get carried away. That was what Hildie had beaten into him over and over. She'd told him of the various stories of the fledgling mages who'd been consumed by their power, crushed by their magic because they believed that they were stronger than it was.

He had to take great care with getting carried away with it.

First he had to understand it.

And then the rest would follow.

Lou turned his attention back to the bubble, to what was happening outside of the protective charm. The cursed crows kept on coming, apparently unabashed by their companions' progress, by their toppling to the floor of the bubble, dying in swathes.

Piling up.

One on top the other.

Beyond them, beyond the irons bars of the gaoler's cart, Lou could make out the sky now, and not just the flock of crows, but the *sky* itself.

The sky was still grey, and dismal, but a thousand shades lighter than the midnight feathers of the crows that had previously blocked out all other light.

He knew that the flock was thinning, that the cursed crows were withdrawing. That those seven guards had gone some way to sate their ravenous appetite.

He watched as the crows continued to patter against the iridescent sheen of the bubble. But they came less frequently now. Whereas before he'd heard a constant shelling, now there was only an offbeat, *pitter-patter*, *pitter-patter*.

It was strange, standing here, in the middle of this protective charm he'd cast himself, and knowing that he'd done it, that when danger had been near he'd managed.

And that it was far more than he ever would've imagined himself capable of in even his wildest of dreams.

In the darkest and dankest of nightmares.

The sky outside of the bubble, outside of the gaoler's cart, got lighter still, so light that he could begin to make out their surroundings, the hundreds of crow corpses scattered about, flattening the long grass. And the corpses of the Royal Guards which, Lou could already see, were pretty much pecked clean of all blood and flesh right down to the bone.

The horses hadn't been spared either, and they resembled beached whales, their ribcages now exposed to the lapping sunlight, their bones soon to be bleached alongside those of their previous masters.

A slight shudder ran up Lou's spine, and he felt a slight frost pass through his blood. He knew that even the ice magic within him was repelled by the sight, and perhaps too by the residue of the dark magic—the fire mage's curse—that had brought these cursed crows down upon them.

And, already, he could feel the light magic, from the protective charm Lou had cast, begin to shake around them, begin to lose its foundation and its strength in the face of such thick and unruly dark magic.

The effect of the protective bubble fading reminded Lou of when he'd head out on the cart, with all the other working hands, along the narrow country lanes, and to the fields.

To Old Man Junth's farm.

It reminded him of light morning mist being burned off in the rising sun, as it slowly ebbed its way up into the sky, and helped itself up to the tops of the trees, for an instant tinting all the foliage in sight in that pink shade.

And he thought of that almost scalding chill he felt on his

cheeks, that stripped away the moisture of his mouth, and the sun rising up and laying its soothing warmth over him, curing him of the night-time cold.

He recalled the animals stirring in the hedgerows: the rabbits hopping, the crickets beginning to chirp, and the larger animals, the deer, or the wild boar, crunching through the thickets, foraging for food in the dawn light.

All those wonders of nature that the sun revealed every day at dawn, and now, Lou felt it in his veins, the stirring of the ice magic in his blood, and he couldn't help but feel a slight shudder rip through him. His heart leap a little in his chest. And he knew that, now he'd started off down the road to becoming an ice mage, he would no longer find solace in those things.

His was the night-time, and the shadows, and the chilly air.

The domain of the ice mage.

As he watched the protective charm fade all round them, and shrivel away into nothingness, he also saw the sun burst through the grey clouds, simply burn them up, and shine down on them, onto the plains, and send up the smells of raw flesh, and damp earth into the air.

And, lingering over everything, smothering it really, he caught the stench of the musk of the cursed crows as they took flight, headed up into the brightening sky.

"So, how d'we get out of here, then?"

Rut's voice took Lou off guard. He had almost forgotten that he was there.

He turned round and looked to him, feeling his mouth turn at the corners in a smile as he took in his friend. It seemed like it had been years, rather than a matter of months, since they'd seen one another.

Properly seen one another.

In the sunlight.

Then Lou processed Rut's words, and realised that he was right. The fact of the matter was that they were still inside the gaoler's cart, still locked away inside this prison cell. And Rut and Sully were still chained up in their respective corners.

Lou shifted over the floor of the cart, listening to the wooden boards squeal beneath his feet, and he headed up to the iron bars, grabbed a hold of them and stared out at the guards' corpses . . . *skeletons* now, really, the crows had consumed most of their uniforms, too, only leaving the slight hint of material on them.

There was no dignity in their deaths.

No matter what the Royal Guards always said about 'dying for the dignity of the Kingdom.' Only now, standing here, peering down at them, did Lou see the fallacy in that statement. If only more of the guards might see what their 'noble' deaths might look like.

Lou stared at what had once been the superior of the guards, and his gaze moved to the man's waist, to his belt, to the Webbing Blade hanging from it, wrapped in cloth in its sheath—surely the guard too had realised that it was too deadly for a mortal to handle—and then Lou shifted his focus to the ring of keys which hung there beside it.

The keys that he knew fit into the lock on the gaoler's cart.

The keys that could let them all go free.

If they couldn't reach the keys then they'd all starve to death here, if someone didn't pass along the road here, on their way to Shildersmoore, to the port.

How long might that be?

A day?

A few days?

Weeks?

Lou glanced back at Sully and Rut, and he knew just by the gauntness of their cheeks, of the bones showing through their grey-tinted skin, and the hollowness of their gazes—Sully in particular—that both of them were already thirsty beyond belief.

Which was to say nothing for hunger.

He stared out over the guards' prostrate corpses, past the jaws of their skulls, latched open in perennial screams, and then he looked beyond the inky-black crows scattered about them, and to the horizon.

There.

Right there.

Couldn't he see movement?

Someone on horseback, closing in on them. Galloping towards them.

His heart fluttered in his chest, and he had to scold himself, force himself not to get carried away.

After all this could all get worse—*much* worse—before it got any better.

For all he knew it might just be another procession of Royal Guards, bringing up the tail of the procession, ready to ride the prisoners on to Shildersmoore, to complete the quest that their companions had already begun.

He stared intently at the approaching figure, narrowed his eyes trying to fathom whether or not the person was dressed in the uniform of the Royal Guards—that whisper-grey colour, the one which he had always known to recognise, on sight, as being synonymous with control, with authority.

With fear.

But the person wasn't dressed in the uniform of the Guards. No they were wearing simply, shabby garments. And the horse certainly wasn't by royal appointment either. It was a mixed breed, a farm pony, meant for a life of back-breaking labour out in the fields.

Lou knew those ponies well.

The way that the person rode, the almost frail way that the pony bounced them around in the saddle, the body almost physically incapable of keeping such a larger beast than itself under control.

And Lou was certain who it was.

Was it?

... It couldn't be, she'd been gone for so long.

And yet he was so sure.

He peered closer, felt the tingle run up his spine, and his blood surge round his veins, the ice magic chill him from the inside once more.

Hildie.

He kept on staring, watching the silhouette bounce on the back of the pony, clop along the muddied track, following the indentations of the gaoler's cartwheels, and the dozens of hoof-marks ingrained in the earth.

And then he realised that it wasn't Hildie at all.

No, it was his sis.

It was Syre.

11

FEVERISH DREAMING

LOU FELT his grip grow tighter and tighter on the Webbing Blade, and the gloom of the king's quarters continue to overwhelm him. The sweat clung to his whole body, and made him shudder in the draught that crept into the room.

He held on tight to the handle of the dagger, but he told himself that this time things would be different, that this time he wouldn't do it at all.

He wouldn't *murder* again.

And even with that matter resolved in his mind, he felt his hands, his arms, working beyond his conscious control, as if manipulated by an invisible hold, and he watched on, simply an observer, as the Webbing Blade rammed down, down and down, into the king's chest.

He listened for the sharp exhale which followed, the gentle way that the ice magic worked itself across the king's skin, freezing him whole, stopping his heart, and jacking the mouth open in the same pose it would strike for the rest of forever.

And then, instinctively, he looked off, into the corner of the room, into the shadows again, and he saw Herimyre there, his sword at his waist, just waiting and watching.

Was there a slight smirk on his lips?

Lou could almost recognise that smirk, it was almost familiar to him. Just thinking about the possessor of that smirk sent shivers through his nerves, and the ice magic in his veins burning through him.

It reminded him of Old Man Junth's son, of Herbert Junth.

It was a cruel smirk, and one that told Lou that this was a man in control, it was like a god watching on as a pawn did his bidding, and happily.

But it was too late.

Lou had already plunged the knife in. He had killed the king, and now, just like every other night in this nightmare, he would have to flee.

And so he did.

Back up on the windowsill, staring out into the palace gardens, and to the drop that awaited him below.

That crow waiting on the branch, staring at him with its glassy eyes, and its indifferent beak.

And then he threw himself downwards, into the gloom.

Into the endless and unstoppable darkness.

Lou's heart caught in his throat. His chest was tight, and he felt fingers gripping his windpipe, preventing the breath from coming.

And he felt the burn of the fingertips, that burn that he knew to recognise as fire magic.

Hildie's magic.

He felt his cheeks billow out, and his heart suddenly remember itself, its role in his body, and begin to hammer again. He glared out into the surrounding darkness, and felt the dank smell of the canvas, of his tent, come back to him.

And somehow it remained in the distance.

He could almost taste the ash at the back of his mouth, though, and it was at the very forefront of his mind. And, almost at the same time, he felt the grip on his throat loosening, and the panic begin to leave his lungs.

But the uncomfortable prickle continued to linger over his skin, and only really began to subside when he felt the weight leave off his bed, and the shape slip through the gloomy interior of his tent, and a spark shoot up from somewhere within the darkness.

The flame licked up in the lantern and bathed the interior of the tent with its orangey glow. Lou blinked in its brightness, in its overwhelming brightness, and just for a second he saw that protective charm he'd cast, that he'd never imagined being able to cast, in his mind's eye. And then he absorbed Hildie, standing out there, coming back at him out of the inside of the tent taking on shape before him.

And he saw her hand, her scarred left hand, that she held down at her side. The one that had been burned away, its flesh half-melted, during her battle with Herimyre.

Before he could think to speak, he glanced around him. He looked to the Webbing Blade, which, just as always when he had the nightmare, was clutched tight to his chest, sending that reas-suring chill pulsing over his skin, like the lapping tongue of a trusted dog at his hand.

And then he looked to his clothes, to his cloak, saw that they lay in their pile at his bed, at his improvised bedroll which he lay on, all that kept him from the simple dirt ground beneath.

Then he looked back to Hildie, but, before he could speak, she stole the march on him, and said, "You've been having nightmares again, haven't you?"

Lou felt a gentle draught, perhaps an early morning breeze, blow through the seams of the tent, and it sent a chill scurrying over his skin, where the sweat still clung to him. Still dazed from the nightmare, he could only manage a nod. A flash of pain passed over his nose. He reached up to touch it and felt a bandage there. With the other hand, he gripped the Webbing Blade all the tighter.

Hildie smiled lightly where she stood, up against the side of the tent, with the lantern in her hand. "You know, it's one thing to sleep with your knife in your hand, but it's quite another to allow someone to get into your sleeping quarters, to get their hands on your throat, to be close enough to kill you."

Lou blinked hard a couple of times, still trying to grow accustomed to the low level of light emanating from the lantern. He could hardly take in what she was saying, his mind still stuck on other things.

Then the world returned to him.

Slowly.

They'd got back, earlier that evening, returned from saving Sully and Rut. The villagers had put on a feast, and they'd all told stories late into the night, drunk home-brewed brandy wine, and ale, although Lou had abstained.

His life was weird enough without intoxicating substances.

A medicine woman had fixed up his nose, told him it wasn't broken, and that it would heal on its own given time.

And then he'd come here, to his tent, fallen down onto his bedroll and allowed sleep to carry him away.

Allowed the nightmares to return.

Lou turned on his side, and eyed Hildie. "Out there, on the plains. I saw you there. You *saved* us."

Hildie's smile widened. "Wow," she said. "I'm flattered, but I'm afraid nothing could be further from the truth. As it happens I've been on the other side of the mountains, I had nothing to do with Syre saving you."

And then it struck Lou, and he recalled.

How Syre had ridden to them, on that pony, that poor, bedraggled pony that surely only wished for a nice, fallow field, and perhaps a wicker basket of apples. She'd ridden it hard up to them, saved them. She'd fetched the keys off the deceased guard and freed them from the gaoler's wagon.

"I . . . I . . ." Lou started, "I managed to do it—I cast the protective charm."

Hildie kept up her smile, and nodded gently. "Good, that's good," she said. "But don't get carried away. It doesn't mean you're a mage. Not yet."

Lou felt the familiar impatience tick within him, that frustrated feeling that he'd been feeling more and more, often when he was in Hildie's presence, and which she'd always demanded he keep a close eye on.

But he couldn't help how he felt.

He knew that the impatience, that roaring ambition to prove everyone wrong, and to meet his destiny head on would always be there, bubbling away beneath the surface.

Who was he to lock it away forever?

Lou decided that it was better to turn matters to other things, to turn the direction of the conversation away from himself, and whether or not he was a mage yet. He squinted in the gleam from Hildie's lantern, and said, "What about you? Where did you go? I just woke up one morning and you were gone."

"But I can see that it did nothing to guard against your heroic deeds, though, you going off to save Sully and Rut."

"There wasn't time," Lou said. "We had to act quickly if we didn't want to miss the chance of saving them."

"And, from what I heard, you almost got yourself into deep trouble."

"But we saved them in the end, that was the important thing."

"With the help of some cursed crows."

Lou simmered away in silence, knowing she was right. Without those cursed crows coming down to bear on the guards he knew that he would've been on the first ship out of Shildersmoore, headed directly to Onderswort.

Leaving Syre, and the rest of his people alone.

Without a leader.

. . . But perhaps that wouldn't have been such a bad thing, because at least they might've been able to find someone more . . . *appropriate* to the task.

Sometimes he couldn't help feeling that he was merely a working hand that'd grown too big for his boots.

Just because there was ice magic running through his veins didn't mean that he would make a mage, as Hildie was constantly reminding him.

Only hard work would get him there.

He eyed Hildie closely, tried to study her unreadable face, to work out just what might be lingering beneath the surface of her expression. But, like always, he came away empty-handed. She was like a blank canvas: impossible to understand or even begin to fathom.

And yet, he saw the slight curl to the corners of her mouth, that sly smile. Finally, it dawned on him. He straightened up in bed, and said, "You! It was you, you were the hobblesman that morning, the one that told us about Sully and Rut."

She grinned wider.

"But why didn't you come to help us?" He felt a slight growing warmth in his chest, a little anger there. "You could've helped us."

She shrugged. "I wanted to see how you'd cope on your own."

"You were watching, weren't you?"

"Maybe."

"Why didn't you step in when they locked me up?" He paused, thought about it. "Or did you? Did you help with the protective charm?"

"No, I had nothing to do with it, and I didn't step in since it seemed like your sister was doing just fine on her own."

Yes, Lou had to admit that Syre had saved them. If she hadn't got a hold of those keys from the superior guard then they would've starved to death even if the crows hadn't managed to pick their bones.

There was something else too, though, now that she was back. He had to know. "Are you gonna stay with us?"

Hildie averted his gaze, and looked down to the flickering flame of the lantern. "I'll be here for a few days."

"But what about my training? You promised you'd help me to understand my magic, to teach me everything you could."

She met his eye, and he felt that fire magic, just below her pupils, smoulder away, almost threaten to melt him from the inside. "You cast the protective charm, and you managed the invisibility charm too. There's nothing left for me to teach you."

Lou lay there, on his side, still staring at her, and trying to work out just what she was saying. He knew that he still had a long way to go, and that she simply couldn't let him go now. She *had* to stay with them.

Or else everything would be in vain.

12

THE ENCAMPMENTS

LOU ACCOMPANIED Hildie around the periphery of the encampments, where the villagers had built up their canvas settlement. The day was just dawning, and the camp was still silent apart from the gentle breeze sending the canvas fluttering like a sea of well-worn flags.

There must've been a thousand or more tents, all set up here, nestled just inside the foothills of the Sable Mountains, kept sheltered from the worst of the elements.

Soon after they'd fled from Ilsnare, they'd set about collecting up the survivors of the other villages, of the villages that Hildie had also burned to the ground.

The ones she'd *had* to burn to the ground to build up her army.

An army that, Lou was sure to insist, would never come into being.

Because, still, the fact remained that he had no intention of his people, of these *good* people, getting themselves wrapped up in the cancer of a magical war.

And they'd all come to settle here. To rest here while they licked their wounds, far from the reach of the Royal Guards, and of the cursed animals. It made him glad that he had the Webbing Blade strapped to his belt, snug in its sheath and ready to be brought out at a moment's notice.

At least Lou *had* thought they'd been far from the reach of the cursed animals until that flock of crows out on the plains had forced him to reconsider.

Would they ever truly be safe until the curse was lifted?

Lou could see a few coils of steam rising up from the camp, where the older women, unable to find sleep, just like him, had set to boiling up water, and beginning to prepare the breakfasts for their families.

Already, he could catch a whiff of those oniony odours, of the broth cooking up on those fires, and he felt his mouth start to water.

Even despite the hearty feast the night before, he could already feel the fatigue of the quest to save Sully and Rut setting in. He supposed it would take several days for him to fully recover.

He reached up to his nose, and carefully, and not without just a little twinge of pain, he peeled the bandage off, discarded it at his feet. He touched the bruised skin, the fresh cut there. That felt better. Exposing his cut to the elements would heal it all the sooner. Just like his ma had always said.

Hildie smiled back at him. "Maybe it hasn't done wonders for your looks, but you certainly look a little more—how should I say? —*heroic*."

"Thanks," Lou said, with the sniff of a chuckle.

Off in the distance, a little further on, he could hear the faint *wail* of the wind blowing through the canyons of the Sable Mountains, and the icy chill that it carried from the snowy peaks. And its cool breath felt reassuring against his cheeks. Against the wound on his nose.

They didn't speak till they'd reached the very edge of the encampments, to where, Lou knew, Hildie believed they would be out of earshot of the villagers. They walked a long while through the lengthening grass, and then to where the grass gave way to the rough texture of rock, springing up on either side of them.

And the foothills proper of the Sable Mountains.

The sun peeked out over the severe, pointed tips of the hills, setting the hardy foliage that dared grow here aflame with its rays. And Lou held up his hand to shield his eyes from the sun's glare. When he slipped a sidelong glance to Hildie he saw she was smiling.

"You just wait," she said. "Soon enough you won't be able to bear the sun at all. It'll cease to be a minor nuisance, and turn out to be the all-out curse on your life."

Lou thought about this for a long while, staring off down into the valley. He had to admit that he noticed this, that the sunlight irritated him, that it caused his blood to thicken and swirl in his veins. And made his heart pound harder.

Or was it just because he was standing close to Hildie?

She smirked a touch and then said, "Don't look so glum about it—don't think that I don't feel the same in the night-time." She turned to the sun, half-closing her eyes as the rays washed over her face. "We've all gotta make sacrifices."

Lou wondered where the sacrifice was in suffering the Moon. At night it was time to sleep . . . at least that was the way that he'd always seen things, from the time when he'd been a working hand, getting up at dawn and working all day in the sun.

The sun had almost been like a source of energy for him, warming up his blood and muscles, and getting him to work. So it was odd to think of it now as an adversary.

He turned to her. "You said you had nothing left to teach me, that it was time for you to move on?"

She remained quiet for a good few moments, and Lou felt the silence thicken between them, and then she said, looking off down into the sun-kissed valley, "I went to go and look for my father." She glanced back at him. "That was where I went to. I climbed up here, headed into the Sable Mountains, wanting to find out anything I could."

"And?"

She shook her head. "I couldn't find anything out at all—it seems like he's headed on without leaving so much as footprints on his way. No one I ran into seemed to know anything."

"So what happens now?"

Again, she stared off down into the valley, seeming to linger over the sun's rays washing the virile sides. Underneath the foliage, just peeking out, Lou could make out the pit-black rock. "Why should you care?" she said, her voice weak, wobbling all over.

"What?" Lou said, and then, studying her face a little harder, he realised that her eyes were filled with tears.

Tears that sparkled in the sunlight.

When Lou spoke again, he made an effort to make his voice warm and soft, understanding. "What're you talking about?"

"The war," she said, staring right ahead, and with her rigid gaze appearing to be attempting to will away her tears, to press them back into the ducts they'd come out of. "You don't care about the war. You're always saying that these people, that the villagers, that they'll never fight." She met his eye briefly. "And that means that they're all doomed. But you're too stupid to see it for yourself."

Lou narrowed his eyes, knowing this routine: she'd lay on the tears, appeal to his better nature, and get what she wanted. Although he noticed this in other women, this was the first time he'd ever observed it in Hildie. In fact, he'd begun to believe that she was incapable of it.

Perhaps not.

He slipped her a sidelong glance. "Why do you think they'll care what I think? If you're so intent on this war of yours then why don't you ask *them*? You burned down their homes, after all."

A flash of anger passed over her eyes, and for a second Lou was almost certain that she was going to lash out, that she was going to catch him with her fingers, and hit him with the fire magic in her fingers.

But she remained still, unfeeling, and he watched as she bunched her fingers into fists, down at her sides. "Because," she said, pointedly, "these people, they see *you* as their leader now. People talk. They know that you led all of these people to freedom, away from the Ilsnare gaol, and that you're a suitable leader—"

Even though he'd considered this himself, thought about this in secret to himself, he chuckled long and hard, breaking through her tirade. "A leader? I'll never be a leader." He shook his head, then chuckled again. "Nah, I think you've got the wrong guy."

When she looked back at him, there was intent in her eyes . . . no, *steel*, and he saw that she was determined that she was correct, and what was more, that Lou knew it to.

At times Lou was ready to swear that she could read his mind.

And perhaps she could.

Although she'd never deigned to teach him the specific charm that the ability required.

He supposed she wanted the upper hand.

Hildie continued, this time her voice low, almost a growl, how Lou often imagined how her father, Ma'reygar, spoke, "These people will do whatever you tell them, Louson, you just need to believe in yourself. And believe me, this war, this *magical* war, it will affect the whole land. They'll make slaves of all of you, of everyone you know. And then, as a mage, they'll force you to join them . . . and as for your sister Syre, they'll make her a slave just like all the others."

Lou felt a slight pang in his chest, and a large sense of outrage, that Hildie had brought his sis into this. What did she have to do with anything?

"If you think you can hide," Hildie continued, "if you can stay here and keep your head down, and that the world will pass you by . . . well you'd be mistaken."

Lou studied her words for exaggeration, and could find none. She was speaking as frankly now as she'd ever spoken to him. And he knew that it was up to him whether or not he chose to listen.

"Once you're a mage, a *fully* trained mage, then these people will certainly listen to you, they'll *follow* you."

Lou stared at the path ahead, losing himself in the pit-black rock that loomed ahead of him, that he knew formed part of the Sable Mountains, that in some way or other connected him, and Hildie, to Ma'reygar right at that moment.

He spoke almost in a whisper. "They'll be afraid of me," he said.

Hildie sniffed a laugh, and it sounded so out of place up there, on the dawning hillside. So much so that it sent a sharp tang through Lou's gut. "Fear can be the greatest weapon you have as a leader," she said.

And then they trudged on in silence.

They carried on walking for around half an hour, perhaps more. When Lou looked up to the sky, to the sun, and tried to tell the time, he guessed it to be around getting-up time. They stopped when they came to a simple wooden bridge, that crossed a large crevice.

He stared down into the blackness, made even more black by the pit-black rock which stretched down either side, which swallowed the sunlight whole. He had always hated heights. He guessed that, at heart, he would always be a working hand—that lover of plains, and open fields.

And that hater of steep drops, and cliff edges.

The bridge stretched out before Lou, and he looked along its length, counting the planks there, for something to do.

So he didn't have to meet Hildie's eye.

He had counted twenty-two planks, and his eyes had almost made it the whole way across, when Hildie turned to him once again.

"This trail," she said, "it leads to Ravensbark, a monastery nestled in the Sable Mountains. About a day's journey from here. Once you cross this bridge you'll be into the thick of the Mountains, among the wind and the snow. Almost no one lives in the Mountains, aside from mythical creatures, and monks."

Lou had the strong sense that she was about to add something more, but that she was holding back. He waited patiently, but then realised that she wasn't going to say anything else. "Right," he said. "It looks very nice, and all, but we probably should be getting off back to the encampments, it's getting on breakfast time."

Hildie turned straight on to him. Her voice was flat, almost toneless. "Once you get to Ravensbark the monks will be able to tell you where to go, they—"

"What?" Lou said. "What're you talking about?"

Hildie gave him a half-smile, and then looked ahead, to the bridge crossing the crevice, and then to the Sable Mountains, looming above them beyond, their pit-black colour almost too much for Lou's eyeballs to absorb.

"You need to ask for Auch'ray."

"Auch'ray? Why? I don't understand."

She gave him a hard, deeply unfeeling glare. "Because he's the one who can help you, who can bring you along further. And, what's more, he's the one who's in possession of the Webbing Bow."

"The Webbing Bow?"

She nodded. "Yes, another of the magical artefacts, the second of the three—"

"I know," Lou said with a slight smile, "but you told me you had no idea where it was located, and now you're telling me that this Ah ... Ah—"

"Auch'ray."

"Yeah, that this Auch'ray, has the Webbing Bow?"

She nodded. "That's just what I'm telling you."

"And you think he'll just give it to me?"

"If you demonstrate yourself to be an able student of his."

Lou stared off at that rickety bridge, what he saw as the entrance to the Sable Mountains, and the road to that place— what had been the name?—Ravensbark, that was it.

He looked back to Hildie, shaking his head. "No," he said. "I've got to stay at the encampments, I need to protect my people."

"Your people *need* that you become a proper mage, so you can properly protect them."

Still, Lou couldn't see himself going through with this. But he was prepared to think it over some. "Come on," he said. "Let's go and get some breakfast."

He made to turn off, to head back down the trail in the direction of the encampments.

Hildie stood firm, arms crossed over her chest. "No," she said. "If you're going then you must go now."

Lou glanced over her, saw that stubborn streak of hers once again taking hold.

"My father," she said, "he's in a hurry to summon his magical army, and if you don't go through with your training, obtain the Webbing Bow, then he'll win. He'll make it to Ilsnare while you're still boiling up beans around a fire."

Lou stared back at her, feeling that anger stir in his stomach again. "Then who'll protect the people while I'm gone?"

"*I* will."

Lou snorted a laugh. "Oh sure, that's right, *you*, the one who burned down their homes in the first place, and I'm supposed to trust you won't do the same while my back's turned?"

To Lou's great surprise, another of those tears sparkled in Hildie's eye, and then rolled down her cheek. He instantly felt like he had hurt her somehow. He *had* been a little brutish with his words. But what other way was there to treat what she had done?

Hildie sank her teeth into her lower lip. "You have my word, Louson Dorf."

Lou stared off past her, to the trail ahead. He felt his mind giving in, his heart doing flips in his chest, and his logical brain going wild about what he was about to say. "If I do this, then you promise that I'll be strong enough to come back here and lead . . . *protect* these people?"

She nodded. "If you're prepared to work hard, and make the journey, then I don't see why not." She parted her lips, thought twice, and then came out with whatever it was she was about to say. "I promise you that I'll take care of your people while you're gone, and then, once you've completed you're training, *then* you can consider whether or not you wish to join up with the magical war." She paused, unfolded her arms, and draped them innocently down by her sides. "Do we have a deal?"

Lou felt his heart stir in his chest, and that brief flash of iciness in his veins. He knew the answer, that whatever had come before, Hildie was advising the right thing now.

And it cut him up inside to know that.

He reached down to his side, and felt for the handle of the Webbing Blade. He felt the cold tingle pass through his fingertips.

Just then the sun peeped out from behind a cloud, and warmed his shoulder blades. Whereas before he'd felt it like a reassuring hand on his back from an elder, now he felt like it was Death himself grabbing him tight, with his bony fingers.

Out ahead, though, the path into the Sable Mountains, was steeped in shadow, where the sun couldn't penetrate, where it was simply absorbed into the pit-black rock.

Once he'd taken the first step it was almost too easy. And then he took the next. And the next. Soon enough he was level again with Hildie, and the start of the bridge.

He stared out ahead of him, to those wooden planks all laid out before him, and then to the pit-black rocks that awaited him on the other side. He glanced back to Hildie, and allowed himself a faint smile. "Guess this is where it starts, huh?"

It happened so quickly.

Hildie tipped forwards, on the tips of her toes, and pressed her lips up against his own.

Lou felt the warmth coming off her lips, and how it seemed to thaw the ice in his own veins. But he couldn't pull away. He just pressed up against her, returning her kiss.

And then, just like that, Hildie leaned back from him, her eyes set in a fresh wave of tears. But she kept her gaze firm, fixed on him.

And he realised, there and then, that she wasn't crying for herself, or for the fate of the world.

She was crying for *him*.

13

ON THE TRAIL TO RAVENSBARK

LOU SET A HARD PACE even though every muscle in his
body seemed to be screaming out for him to stop and take a
rest. For him to take on some sustenance. For him to take a drink
of water, or for him to eat something.

But the fact was that there was nothing *to* eat, nothing *to* drink.

He hadn't passed so much as a stream as he made his way
along the mountain pass. Not since he'd left the encampments
behind.

A day's journey, that was what Hildie had said. Did he have
any reason not to trust her?

He thought back to that kiss, to her lips pressed against his.
How soft they'd been, and slightly moist. And how her fire had
sent tingles through his bloodstream, right the way to the centre of
his heart.

And how, already, he missed that feeling.

What was it that she'd said all that time ago? About how as he
grew stronger in his powers, as she grew stronger in hers, that it

would become almost impossible for them to so much as be in the same room as one another?

He hoped she'd been exaggerating.

As he walked on, he listened to the crunch of the trail beneath his boots, and the rap of his heart on his throat as he clambered up the ever-steepening slopes. He could feel the sweat seeping out of all parts of him too, and taste its saltiness on his tongue.

When he breathed in he was glad for the fresh mountain air. It was a freshness he'd never felt before, that he'd never had a chance of experiencing out on the plains, where the air grew stale as the sun beat down on the fields, and the wind swept the corn dust up into the air.

And that was to say nothing of being back in the town, how the whole place had stunk of a latrine . . . although he guessed that was just how the encampments smelled now.

As he carried on his way, he could feel his stomach churning, desperately trying to find some nourishment from the feast he'd consumed the night before. If only he could find a stream, drink some water, it might take his mind off his hunger. If only for an hour or so.

When he didn't think about food or water, he thought about Syre, and regretted how he hadn't got the chance to speak with her, to wish her goodbye. But he trusted that Hildie would explain.

Trusted? Really? Was that the right word for her now?

He found it almost impossible to think of Hildie, to picture her in his mind without thinking back to that kiss of theirs only hours ago, on the bridge. He wondered if it had been a ploy, some kind of act.

But, searching himself, thinking it over, turning it round in his mind again and again, he simply couldn't see it.

One thing was for certain, with several hours out on the moun-

tain trail, and the sun beginning to dip over the crest of the mountains, he would have no chance of turning back, of going back
home now.

Not unless he wished to endure the sub-zero night tempera-
tures out here on the mountain trail. He had come more than
halfway now, got more than halfway to Ravensbark.

He was sure of it.

And yet he wished that he would get there a little sooner.
Because every time he lifted his foot to take another step, he felt
all the muscles in his leg lock up, almost become unresponsive.
And he could already feel the numbness of fatigue setting in.

What he would give for a nice, clean, private room with a
warm fireplace.

That was most likely wishful thinking seeing as, when he
thought about monks, he never considered comfort of any kind.

They were all about hardship and functionality.

No, he wouldn't find any comfort there.

The Moon had already risen above as Lou rounded the next
turn of the mountain path, to be confronted with an enormous
structure. Nothing short of a huge, charcoal-shaded fortress
sticking out from the side of the mountain.

Ravensbark.

Even when he breathed in he was sure he could smell and
taste the charcoal there. And he was almost certain that he'd taken
a wrong turn. That this place couldn't *possibly* be a monastery.

It just seemed so . . . so *opulent*.

But where else might it be? There hadn't been any other way to
turn on this mountain trail, unless Hildie had misled him, sent
him walking down the wrong road.

And he couldn't quite completely discount that eventuality.

He kept himself close to the side of the mountain, noticing

that the path grew more narrow here, and that the drop to his left seemed to get steeper.

But he couldn't help glancing up, every couple of steps, just to confirm that, *really*, this place existed.

And that he was headed right for it.

His hopes of a long-deserved rest and good-time comfort came back to him in droves.

Night had fallen by the time Lou had hoisted himself up the charcoal-coloured steps, and up to the gigantic oaken doors which marked the entrance to Ravensbark. The doors must've been taller than at least three or four men, all standing on one another's shoulders.

A hefty brass knocker hung down off the door, and Lou reached out, gave it a couple of hard raps. And he listened to the *boom* resound throughout the entrance hall and, seemingly, through the entirety of the as-yet-unseen monastery.

Lou waited, staring at the wood weave of the door, noting the ravens carved into its design. He felt his chest prickle a little. The ravens reminded him of the crows. Of *the* crow from his dream. And yet, even though he felt uncomfortable standing there, before that towering door, his hunger and thirst were such that he was determined he was willing to stand here until the end of time.

He could smell a mixture of charcoal and meat, floating underneath the huge door, wafting its way up his nostrils. And he hoped the monks had plenty to share.

From within, he heard the *slap* of footsteps, and then, hearing a slight groan of exertion on the other side of the door, he watched the door heave back in on itself, its hinges screeching out as it went.

Torchlight glowed out from within the hallway, leaving the figure standing in the doorway almost as a silhouette. At least for the few seconds it took Lou's eyes to get adjusted. And then he saw him just fine.

A man . . . a *boy* really, a few years younger than Lou and about seventeen or eighteen. He had crisp blond hair and fragile features. And shining, icy blue eyes. He seemed a little nervous in the way that he hung back from the entrance, stood to one side in invitation for Lou to enter.

Lou waited for the boy to say something, but he just kept as silent as before. So he decided that it fell to him to break the silence. "Uh, this *is* Ravensbark?"

The boy nodded slightly.

"Right, then, please allow me to introduce myself. My name is Louson Dorf, and I am an *ice* mage. I'm currently on the way to seek out Auch'ray, a famous mage, and I was told that I might expect hospitality here, in Ravensbark, before I continue on with my journey tomorrow, I—"

Without a word, the boy shifted off along the corridor, heading off into the brighter glow of torchlight.

Deeper into Ravensbark.

Lou stared after him for a while, for a second or so struck by the rudeness of the boy, that he hadn't even thought to greet him, let alone respond to him. And now he was walking off and leaving him here, at the entrance hall to what, for want of a better word, was a stranger's home.

Lou watched as the boy slipped out of sight, back around the turn of the corridor, and then he glanced back over his shoulder, and realised that the front door to the monastery was still wide open.

He looked back out, to the Sable Mountains, to their sooty shapes in the glow of moonlight, and he looked back along the path which snaked round the forms of the mountains, and he thought about how he'd come all that way.

And without any food or water.

Could he make it back to the encampments if he really tried?

No, and it would be the mark of a madman to even try.

So why was he still considering it?

"Louson Dorf."

A voice drifted along the corridor, thick and hard, and gruff.

It sent a tingle up Lou's spine, and he turned round slowly, and looked in the direction it had come from.

Silhouetted in the torchlight coming from along the corridor, the monk looked quite imposing. Lou almost thought he was a towering hulk of a man, perhaps a clear head and shoulders taller than he was.

As the monk approached him, he heard the thin *slap* of the man's sandals against the stone slabs of the floor. And, as the monk came closer, he seemed to grow smaller in stature, and as Lou caught more details of his face, he saw that he really wasn't the imposing presence he had expected.

Lou realised that he'd been gripping tightly to the handle of the Webbing Blade, and he had to make a conscious effort to rip his fingertips back from it, and to hold them, rather unquietly, down at his side.

The monk had chubby, rounded cheeks, and loose lips. His skin seemed to sheen in the glow from the torchlight. But all this jolly aspect wasn't to say that he was smiling.

In fact, he had a face like thunder.

The monk came nearer still, and Lou remarked on how it was impossible to make out his shape from the cloak that he wore. He might've been a rolling todge of a man, or he might've had a body akin to a piece of wood whittled within an inch of its life.

Whatever it was, Lou found himself taking a step back, a step back towards the front door of the monastery, back towards the moonlight and the Sable Mountains.

The monk kept coming, and soon enough Lou had to stop, he felt the stone hearth step behind his ankle, and knew he could go no further without all-out turning round and fleeing. When the monk spoke his words were cool, and strung with tension. "*Who sent you here, mage?*"

Lou felt the words stick in his throat, and his hand, unconsciously, reached down his side and felt for the handle of the Webbing Blade. And he savoured the cooling influence, that slight, reassuring, chilly glow that emanated from it. "Hildie," he said, and then realising that he'd used the short form of her name, he added, "Hilda. Daughter of Ma'reygar."

The monk retained his earlier intensity for a few seconds, and then he blinked once, then twice, and everything about him seemed to soften. He sank back on his heels, and his eyes drifted back in their sockets as he appeared to consider this.

His deliberations apparently done with, he glanced back up at Lou and said, "She's a friend of yours, is she?"

Lou nodded.

"Yes, I know Hildie, a good girl. One of the good ones."

Lou had the urge to butt into the conversation, and to explain to him about how she'd burned down half of the villages on the plains of Ilsnare. But he decided that he had to be diplomatic right now. He had to keep his lip buttoned if he hoped to find the refuge he sought.

The monk met Lou's eye, and Lou saw the briefest twinkle there. "Been in a fight, have you?"

Lou reached up for his nose, felt the healing skin there, and managed a smile. "Something like that."

The monk grew stern once more. "You do realise the risk that we take on in offering mages hospitality here at Ravensbark, do you not?"

Lou thought about answering in the affirmative, but rethought it at the last second. The way he saw it, he was much better off being honest with this monk. Something about him told him that he had the same ability Hildie seemed to have.

That he could find out just what Lou was thinking without needing him to say as much.

Lou shook his head.

The monk let loose a long sigh, a sigh that seemed as natural and as long-cultivated as the Sable Mountains that surrounded the monastery. "Then at least you're not that far along in your training." He stared deep into Lou's eyes. "You're not yet a *fully-fledged* mage?"

"No, sir," Lou said.

The monk nodded to himself, and then glanced off over his shoulder, back along the well-lit corridor.

Lou felt a mountain breeze blow from behind him, and he was sure he could feel a few flakes of snow carried along with it as they landed on his skin, froze themselves into his skin. And he caught a whiff of that meat.

Roast pork.

He was sure of it.

He could just picture the pig in his mind now, stuck on its spit, an apprentice monk slowly turning it over the crackling embers, occasionally stopping to throw over some seasoning or other. Up here, in the Sable Mountains, they must have some extremely exotic herbs and garnishes. He was sure it would be a terrific feast.

If he was *welcome* here, that was.

The monk looked to Lou, and then a faint smile appeared on his lips, to reveal his slightly yellowed teeth, and the well-worn smile lines around his eyes. He lurched forwards and clasped Lou on the shoulder. "Fine, then, *Louson*, was it?"

"That's right," Lou replied.

"We'll get you sorted out with a room for the night, don't you worry about that." He paused, glanced back at the open door, to the Sable Mountains looming large in the moonlight, and then he clapped Lou on the shoulder. "And don't think I haven't noticed you sniffing out the feast we've got cooking up."

Lou allowed himself a brief smile in return to the monk.

"Just one thing, before we go," the monk said.

"What, sir?"

"Shut that bloody great door, would ya?"

14

A FRESH ACQUAINTANCE

T HE MONK who had greeted Lou at the door turned out to be the *Abbot* of Ravensbark. And his name, as he told Lou, was Damon Shriversmyth. He promised him a bed for the night if Lou would promise, in turn, to be gone before sunrise the next day.

With no other option, Lou accepted. After all, he had no intention of encroaching on the monks' hospitality. He just needed some sustenance so that he might get going the next day, to go and meet the man who was to be his mentor.

To go and meet with Auch'ray: the possessor of the Webbing Bow.

The bedspread was extremely soft—*silk*, Lou was almost sure. A log-burning stove crackled away embedded into one wall of the room, and he felt its comforting glow warm the room. The monk who had prepared his room had also left a wooden jug filled with water, which Lou had soon drained, and yet it had done nothing to ease his hunger pangs.

More than anything he was looking forwards to the feast that awaited him.

A little while later, after Lou had left the Webbing Blade on the pillow of his bed—as Damon had requested he do, not wanting the magical artefact in the dining hall—he heard the familiar *slap* of sandals making their way up along the corridor. And then a pair of faint, almost unintelligible, knocks.

He asked the knocker to come in.

The blond monk, the same as one as before, peeped round the door, and said, in a high-pitched, rather squeaky voice, "Dinner's served, sir."

The monk made to duck back out of sight, but Lou called out to him, doing his best to make his voice a little crooked, and rough . . . in short, as mage-like as he could make it.

"Listen here," Lou said. "What was all that about back in the entrance hall?"

The tiny monk's eyes seemed to bulge in their sockets, and his complexion went just about as pale blond as the fine hairs which made up his eyebrows. "The entrance hall, sir?"

"Why didn't you speak with me?"

"Oh, uh, sir, you see, it's what Abbot Shriversmyth tells us to do. We're not to waste words while we're apprentices." His eyes wandered Lou's room, going over the oak furniture: the four-poster bed, the trunk at the foot of the bed, and finally coming to rest on the wardrobe standing up in the corner of the room. His eyes then suddenly snapped back on Lou. "And whenever we have unfamiliar guests, such as yourself." His eyes wandered beyond Lou once again, and Lou knew he was staring at the Webbing Blade, lying on the pillow of the bed. "*Magical* guests, then we must take extreme care."

Lou saw that the blond monk was trapped, that while he

wished for nothing more than to be excused, to skitter off down the corridor, back to his quarters, or to wherever he hid out, he also knew that his manners prevented him leaving until Lou took the decision to excuse him.

But Lou wanted to play a little longer. And he wanted to know more about Ravensbark. It seemed to him that he had more chance of getting useful information out of this young monk, than he would out of Damon . . . or should he really be calling him Abbot Shriversmyth?

"How long have you been here?" Lou said.

The blond monk widened his eyes as if Lou had just told him that he intended to run him through with the Webbing Blade. "Just over a year, sir."

"And how did you come to be here?"

The monk's eyes twitched from Lou's gaze and then bounced back around the room. His voice struck a lower register when he replied. "My parents, sir, they sent me to be here."

"And how did that come about?"

"Magic, sir."

"Magic?"

"Yes, sir."

"I don't understand."

The monk got all skittish all of a sudden, more so than before. He began tapping his fingers against the edge of the door, and he stared into the flames of the log-burning stove.

Lou felt like a cat he'd once saw with a mouse. How it had got the mouse cornered, up against a stonewall. And how he'd watched the cat release the mouse, only for it to try and patter away and escape in some direction for a few seconds before the cat caught its tail in its mouth and replaced it back where it had started.

But there was still more he wanted to know.

However, this time, the monk continued without needing Lou's prompting. "I come from Dweldwock, sir. It's a village on the other side of the Sable Mountains. A pit, sir. A mine. That's what the main industry there is."

Dweldwock. That name sparked some recognition in Lou's mind. He thought about it some more. Dweldwock? Yes, that was certainly a place he'd heard of before.

And then it struck him, and he remembered those hobblesmen, the men who had come to Endmere and shown their paintings. The ones with the *pit-black* tones. *They* had been from Dweldwock.

Lou smiled thinly. "Yes, I've met some men from Dweldwock, they came to my village once. Painters, both of them."

For the first time, a spark seemed to spring up in the young monk's eye, and he flashed a smile at Lou. "Arknaught and Gradleton."

"Yes," Lou said, feeling the glow of recognition take him over. "I remember now, those were their names."

The monk was grinning hard now, showing off all those young, strong, blindingly white teeth of his.

Lou realised this was his opportunity, that he'd managed to get the boy to feel a little more familiar in his company. Now was his chance to learn more about the monks. About *what* Ravensbark was at all.

"And you said magic sent you here, why was that?"

The monk's smile faded a little, and that matted quality returned to his eyes. "They found the magic in my veins, sir. *Ice* magic. And they sent me away. It's a traditional place, Dweldwock, sir. Not much place for any of that magic stuff, sir. Enough as it goes with the magical beasts that roam the passes, that eat a good measure of our villagers."

Lou stuck out his lower lip, and closed one eye. "But, surely if it's true, that you have magical blood in your veins, then one of your parents would have had the same? Why didn't they send your parents away?"

The monk gave Lou the glimmer of a smile, and Lou was sure that there was a slight wicked edge to it. "My mother, sir, people of the village say that she took another man. A *mage*, sir. And that's how I got the magical blood in me, sir. My brothers and sisters, see, when the monks came to our village, to search for the magical blood, they didn't find none in them, sir. None at all. But they did find it in me, sir, so they brought me here, to Ravensbark."

Lou was on the cusp of asking another question when his stomach came to bear on the conversation. It gurgled long and hard, quivering him right down to the bone. And when he glanced over to look at the young monk, to meet his eye, he saw that he was smiling. And soon Lou was too.

And their smiling graduated into a mutual chuckle.

On their way through the winding stone corridors of Ravensbark, headed for the dining hall, the young monk told Lou that his name was Flucknor Arch . . . although it was prohibited for monks to use their surnames, their previous family names, once they'd been taken on at Ravensbark. And so he was only known as Apprentice Flucknor now.

And, in any case, Arch wasn't the surname of his father.

Not his *real* father.

Flucknor reeled through the history of Ravensbark, and told

him about how it had been founded by a pair of monks, one of ice magic and the other fire, and how they'd built up the whole ethos of the place as a set of scales, a meticulously balanced place which sat right between all the graduations of magic: between fire and ice, light and dark.

And for that reason, Lou learned, the monks had to be careful of which influences it allowed within its walls. Flucknor insinuated to Lou that if he hadn't mentioned his relationship to Hildie, then Abbot Shriversmyth . . . Damon, might well have thrown him out for a night exposed to the elements in the Sable Mountains.

And if Lou had been any further along in his training as an ice mage, then Abbot Shriversmyth might well have thrown Lou out all the same, in a bid to protect the neutrality of Ravensbark.

He told Lou about how Ravensbark existed to bring up monks in elemental magic, and to educate them in the very strongest of the protective charms. And that any monk who found himself caught going down either the path of the light, or the dark, or the fire or the ice, would soon be exiled from Ravensbark.

Because Ravensbark existed as the perpetual marker between all four strands of magic, and because of its position it often found itself open to attack from those who wished to upset the balance of the natural world.

And Lou began to see that what Hildie had told him, what Ma'reygar was hoping to achieve, would mean just that for Ravensbark.

But he kept those thoughts to himself.

As they crept closer to the dining hall, and the roast pig wafted on the thick, slightly stale air of the monastery, his gut quivered with hunger and his mouth watered with a new fury. And he felt his tunic becoming damp with sweat as he anticipated the feast awaiting him.

They had only stepped in through the arch of the dining hall when, with a flittish goodbye, Flucknor rushed off, hugging the wall of the dining hall and lost himself among a bunch of the monks, among those hundreds and hundreds of brown cloaks, and bald heads.

Lou stood lingering in the doorway, not quite sure where he should go, until he heard the familiar tones of Damon, calling to him from the other side of the hall, over the *scrape* of cutlery and blabber of conversation.

15

AN UNWELCOME GUEST IN RAVENSBARK

LOU PICKED HIS WAY through the tables and tables of monks. The tables were all made up of the same oak he had in his bedroom here, and although the design was simple, and with just roughly drawn-together benches pulled up to the tables, it all carried the air of weightiness, and of something that was, well, immovable.

Or, at the very least, difficult to shift.

Damon had already taken his seat back at his bench and, Lou saw, he was sawing away at his roast pork, slicing it off before dabbing it in what looked like a puddle of thick gravy. Lou noticed that there was a space on the bench beside Damon, and realised that this was the place he was most likely supposed to take up.

As he approached the table, and his vision seemed to get totally consumed with that roast pork all laid out there, and steaming away up into the dining hall, he felt his gut quiver yet again, and his mouth salivate so much that he was almost worried that he might drown.

He sat down on the bench, hearing its sturdy oak wood creak beneath him as it accommodated itself to his weight, and he waited there, staring at the clay plate before him, and the cutlery at the side.

He was wondering what to do next, and was on the point of slipping Damon a side glance, breaking this frosty silence that had somehow sprung up between them, when he heard that same *slap* of sandals over his shoulder, and saw Flucknor standing there, holding a joint of pork speared onto a blade.

He didn't show off any sign that they'd spoken in confidence on their way to the dining hall, which was to say that he slipped the pork off its blade in silence, and without so much as meeting Lou's eye.

Before Lou even got the chance to thank him, Flucknor had already slipped the pork off the blade and disappeared back into the mass of brown cloaks and hushed conversation.

Lou looked down at his piece of pork and he felt his stomach rumble long and hard. He noticed Damon glancing to him out of the corner of his eye.

Damon spoke to him, still busying himself with cutting up his own pork, clearly not intending to meet Lou's eye. "So," he said. "I understand you're off to see Auch'ray."

"Yes, sir."

"Hmm," Damon said, still very much concentrating on slicing up his meat rather than the content of the conversation. He popped in the next slice, and spoke as he chewed. "Bit of a moody bastard, that man."

Lou flinched a little. He'd noticed a little earlier, when Damon had asked him to shut the front door, that there was something about Damon that just didn't sit right with his perception of what a monk should be. But who was he to say what a monk should be like? It wasn't like he had ever met one.

Lou, though, tried to keep his tone as polite as he could, as free from confrontation as he could manage. He was, after all, a guest here. "Is that so?" Lou said, cutting up his own pork, already smelling those waves of meat blow up his nostrils, and tickle his gut all the more.

"Mm," Damon said, reaching across the table to refill his flagon with, what Lou saw to be, ale. He poured it into his flagon till the ale overflowed the rim, and then, without meeting Lou's eye, offered it to him.

"No, thank you," Lou said, with a smile.

Damon shrugged and replaced the jug of ale. Some of its froth burst over the rim and splashed onto the table. But none of the monks seemed to mind. And Lou guessed this was just normal.

They slipped into silence once again, and Lou took it upon himself to break it. "What's 'moody' about Auch'ray?"

"Just like all ice mages, you know, night owls the lot of them." Damon met Lou's eye briefly and made a guesture with his finger at his temple. "Gets to make them a bit crazy, that's all." He turned back to his pork. "And moody too."

Lou felt a lump form in his throat, and he reached forwards for the flagon of water he hadn't been aware that anyone had poured for him. Had Flucknor returned while he'd had his back turned and delivered him the water?

He took a sip of water, but the lump remained in his throat, and he guessed that he just had to come out with what he wanted to say to Damon. But before he got the chance to speak, Damon beat him to it.

"Strange for an fire mage to befriend an ice mage, don't you think?"

Lou thought this over for a moment, and he couldn't help also thinking of their farewell, back on the bridge. And the softness of Hildie's lips. He hadn't told Damon what kind of mage he was, even, but he guessed that the very fact that he was searching out Auch'ray made that obvious.

And that he'd seen the Webbing Blade.

Or, just as likely, and if what Flucknor said was true, then he was certain Damon had enough magic of his own to sniff out the magical class of others.

Why else would he have become Abbot at Ravensbark?

"Me and Hildie were thrown together really," Lou said.

"That so?"

"Yes."

Although Lou didn't want to look Damon straight in the eye, he caught, in the corner of his vision, a slight smile pass over Damon's lips as he said, "And how many fires did she start this time?"

Lou felt the pain wrench in his gut, even past the pork churning away, and being digested there. He caught images of his ma and his pa in his mind's eye, and found it tough to shake them. But he knew he had to act mature. He wasn't some woe-betide orphan. He was a fully grown man.

A man who would one day be a mage.

Lou even managed a smile to match Damon's as he replied. "She burned down my village, and most of those along Capital Road." He paused as he considered how much more information to spill, and decided that, whatever else Damon was, he was a person that Lou could trust. "The survivors are all camped out, nestled just into the foothills of the Sable Mountains."

Damon's cutlery landed down on his clay plate with a clatter.

He turned to Lou with his brows furrowed and his lips slightly parted. Lou watched as he wet his lips with his tongue several times before he caught hold of the courage to actually speak the words. "She did *what*?"

Lou retained his composure. Even through all that ashen air, and that fogging smog, those crackling flames destroying everything he'd ever known. Killing his parents. He managed to keep a distance from the whole matter, and finally felt that, for the first time in their acquaintance, he had the upper hand.

He knew more than the monk.

"You heard me," Lou said, popping another slice of pork past his lips.

Damon seemed stuck in wide-eyed shock for several moments, and when he came out of it he got caught in a fury of blinking, as if he could hardly believe the air in front of his nose. And then he cast his glare down to his clay plate. "I had no idea," he said, and then half-turned to Lou. "And your family?"

"Dead, aside from my sister."

Damon gave him a steely smile and then, the smile quickly slipping from his lips, he snatched up his flagon of ale and drank it all down in a single gulp. When he replaced the flagon back on the table before him, making a hollow, woody note as it landed, he looked long and hard into Lou's eyes and said, "So it's true then. She's begun to take after her father."

Lou thought of a thousand ways he might respond, about telling Damon how Hildie believed that there was a magical war coming. But, somehow, he was sure that Damon already knew of the global shifts, and that this one, this rudely *personal* matter was far more important to him at this moment in time.

But all Lou had done was tell the truth.

And all it had done for Lou was confirm to him that there was no one, not in the whole of the world, who knew—who *really* knew—Hildie.

16

LEAVING RAVENSBARK

FLUCKNOR WOKE Lou early the next morning. He did so with a slight shake of him, rocking him a little through his thick, smothering silk blankets.

Lou came to fairly easily, and he remarked to himself about how this had been the first night he'd passed since . . . since he'd *killed* that he hadn't had the nightmare. And he wondered whether it had something to do with the sanctity of Ravensbark. If there was something here in the mountain air.

He had no need to ask about it.

In fact, he was reasonably sure that he felt it himself.

After Flucknor had brought him a hearty breakfast of eggs and bacon and a cup of herb-infused tea that surged right to Lou's brain, woke him up instantly, he made to get ready to leave on his journey.

He wasn't entirely sure what he'd expected, after all he'd only come here to spend the night. But he had thought that Damon would at least see to getting up from his bed only to ensure that

Lou had actually left Ravensbark, and that he wasn't intending to linger there for several days.

But there was no sign of the Abbot, and Flucknor was his only company as he proceeded through the stone corridors of Ravensbark.

He realised, as he followed Flucknor, that they were headed down several spiral staircases, going deeper and deeper into Ravensbark. He felt a slight tingle of fear pass over his skin as he wondered whether he might be falling into a trap.

Because, the thing was, now Damon had decided that Hildie might not be one-hundred-per-cent trustworthy, Lou had lost the vote of confidence too.

But, Lou thought somewhat haphazardly, at least he hadn't slit anyone's throat while they slept. Surely that would find him get at least a tiny line of credit with the Abbot.

Or not.

They emerged through the cloisters of Ravensbark, an area open to the shining morning sun. And, Lou realised, peering out over the walls, that they were positioned right on the mountain's edge.

Flucknor hurried on, his pace not at all affected by the looming drop below. That drop into that pit-black rock, that went all the way down, to that tiny scribble of a river which ran through the valley.

If Lou breathed in hard he was sure he could almost taste the spring water down there.

They carried on along a narrow corridor which opened out onto the valley below, showing off the steep slopes. And Lou felt his stomach plummet away from him, and thought himself in danger of losing his breakfast.

As it turned out, he did taste his eggs and bacon coming back up to tickle his throat.

Which was to say nothing for the herb-infused tea.

But they skirted the mountain trail and emerged into another room, stone like the rest of Ravensbark, and it stunk heavily of horse flesh. And only once Lou's eyes had grown accustomed to the gloom did he realise that those gently swaying shapes close to him, those slight blubbering exhales of air were in fact horses in their stables.

That was where they were.

They were in the stables.

Lou wanted to ask Flucknor why they'd come down here, but Flucknor continued to patter along, his sandals still slapping against the stone slabs as he led him along. And then they reached a pair of horses, already tacked-up, and catching a quick sleep before their, apparently, long journey ahead.

Only then did Flucknor turn round to glance over Lou, with a slight smile on his face. "Abbot Shriversmyth instructed me to lead you along the road to Auch'ray's lodging." His smile lost a little of its intensity, and his voice dipped a little in tone. "I can't wait for you, of course, who's to know how long you shall spend there with the master, but he thought it better for you to make the journey in a day on horseback, rather than the three or four days it would take you to reach your destination on foot."

Lou thought this over and tried to recall exactly what it was that Hildie had said to him. Hadn't she said it would be a short journey from Ravensbark to arrive at Auch'ray's home?

Or perhaps he was just imaging things.

Now that he'd seen that expression of surprise all laid out on Damon's face, his surprise at what Hildie had done, he was sure that it had also had an impact on him too. That he'd begun to suspect every little thing Hildie said to him.

But the question was, did he suspect her kiss too?

Had that been genuine, or simply a calculated act of deception?

It made little difference now. All he could do was keep going. And now that he had Flucknor to ride alongside him it made him feel much better.

And so, with a brief glance to the apprentice monk, he smiled back, and they both took to the saddle and set off along the mountain pass.

Today, more than ever, Lou felt the sun weighing him down, and he was glad to have the horse to carry him on his way. Who was to say whether or not he might've made that three- or four-day journey if he'd only had the boots on his feet?

Had Hildie simply planned this journey in the hope that he might die?

He liked to think not, and in any case, if she had, then why send him off in the direction of Ravensbark, where there was the hope of refuge? Why wouldn't she have just sent him off in the direction of some unbegotten wilderness where she could be sure of him dying of thirst or hunger, or both?

He swayed on the horse's back, and he felt his gut clenching and unclenching over and over again. He thought back to the rich food from the night before, to that sweet desert he'd had after all the meat courses—after another three helpings of pork —and he began to wonder whether it had truly been a good idea.

Hadn't he heard about the poor judgement of eating like a king on an empty stomach?

But the feast had been truly irresistible, even now, seated on the horse, and feeling more nauseous in the sun by the second, he admitted that much to himself.

They climbed and climbed in the late morning until they reached a flat peak, and there Flucknor dismounted his horse, before helping Lou down from his own—Lou guessed that Flucknor had noted either his pale complexion, or the light groans he had been making with each lurch of the horse.

Flucknor broke out a saddlebag which turned out to contain a canister of water, and some bread rolls stuffed with the pork from the night before.

While Lou had very little urge to eat any more of that pork, or to be reminded of the pork that continued to swirl about in his stuffed-full belly, he accepted the sandwiches, hoping they might make him feel better.

Either the sandwiches or the shade from the sun did wonders for his aspect, and he felt his strength slowly coming back to him. Oh sure, he still had the aching muscles, and fatigue still seemed to have most of his nerves in its vicelike grip, but he could go on.

And that was the most important thing.

In the afternoon the sky clouded over, and Lou felt a, not unwelcome, chill enter the air. He looked about him, getting a strange stirring feeling inside his chest, that feeling that somehow someone was watching him.

But there was nothing to see, just the Sable Mountains on all sides, with their pit-blackness, the blackness of the mines of

Dweldwock, Flucknor's hometown. Just looking too long at that shade of black, Lou was sure, would turn him crazy. It was like staring into some all-consuming abyss, and losing your soul amongst it all.

Thinking back on it, Lou had difficulty remembering whether or not the swirling gale or the hail had started first. But he was certain that it was the hail that drove them into the side of the mountains, so that they might get out of its range.

The hail pinged down, off the path, and rolled down the pit-black cliffs and into the valley below. Lou could see the hail splashing into the stream which ebbed through the floor of the valley, and saw the hail piling up on its banks.

It took him by surprise when Flucknor got down off his horse, and stood alongside it, waiting for Lou to catch up. He supposed that they were set for a break. After all, the sun was slipping off behind the mountains now, and it would be dark before too long.

The cloud didn't help, of course. It had made everything grey. And set the whole landscape in a kind of twilight glow.

Lou felt that familiar chilly tingle pass along his hand and he instinctively reached for the handle of the Webbing Blade, for the comfort he found there. And he grasped the handle tight, feeling that frostiness stronger than he'd ever felt it before.

Even more than the burning cold he'd first felt when he'd tried to take the dagger in his hand.

Flucknor gazed about the skies, his eyes darting about once more, and clearly uncomfortable. But he did manage a nervous smile, which he directed at Lou as he said, "I'm afraid this is as far as I can go. I must take the horses back from here."

Lou thought this over for a few moments, and then, looking out into the gloom which rolled thick and fast over the mountains, and down their sides, he knew that Flucknor was right.

He looked to him, with a new warm fondness worming through his heart. He held out his hand, and Flucknor took it, and gave it a brisk shake. A much brisker shake than Lou ever would've imagined from such a young, frail-looking adolescent. And he supposed that there might well be, very much like in his own case, a much steelier interior to Flucknor than the one that he projected to the world.

Because, after all, Lou knew that if things had been different, if monks had come to Endmere, he might very well have ended up as an apprentice monk himself. There wasn't all that much different between himself and Flucknor, he knew that.

Both had ice magic running through their veins.

Lou stood still, back pressed against the mountain edge, grasping his cloak around him, desperately trying to preserve some semblance of the warmth within his body. But it seemed to be futile. The gales just blew too hard, and too frosty.

He watched as Flucknor ebbed his way back along the mountain pass, riding the first horse, and the second, the one which Lou had ridden, trailing on a rope at his hind. And he kept on watching after them until they disappeared off around the corner and out of Lou's sight.

As Lou pressed on, made his way up the ever-inclining mountain path, and into the very claws of the hailstorm, he hoped and prayed that Flucknor would get back to Ravensbark safely.

And, deep within himself, he somehow knew that he would.

Lou brought the hood of his cloak up to cover everything except for the narrow slit which he needed for his eyes. The hail and flurries of snowflakes were so thick and so relentless now that he could hardly see the ground in front of his feet.

The shivers tore right through him, shaking him to the bones, and rattling his teeth.

He was sure that more than once he heard his teeth crack from his shudders and at one point, as he navigated a particularly precarious edge, he was certain his blood would ice over once and for all, that he would be left in a block of ice here on the mountain path.

But then, up ahead, he saw hope.

He saw a pair of torches, guiding him onwards.

A pair of torches seeming to hang straight off the rock face, and to entice him forwards.

A fresh urgency entered his stride, and he cast off all thoughts of the freezing cold he was enduring and shoved himself forwards, chewing on his tongue, riding the pain. And then he came up against the rock face, the space between the two torches.

And there was nothing.

Nothing at all.

17

SEEKING OUT A MASTER

LOU PEERED UPWARDS, straight up the rock face.

There was nothing to see. The pit-black rock just towered over his head, and then into the falling gloom of the evening, and into the rising fog.

At least he had some cover from the rapidly falling hail, though. That was something.

He could feel the sandwich still stirring in his stomach, still not quite sitting right with him. And that pork scent seemed to be permanently stamped upon his tongue. He listened to the continuing pattering of the hail, as it smashed into the Sable Mountains and then rolled down into the valley that fell away below him.

Down into what was now nothing short of an abyss.

No longer could he make out the pleasantly curving stream at the base of the valley.

Now it was only fog and darkness.

Lou pressed his back up against the rock face and peered all around him, glad to find that he still had the pair of torches attached here. And the assumption that followed: that Auch'ray's home couldn't be far. He backed up a little, to bask in the vague warmth of the torches. And he felt the prickle of the ice magic in his veins protest.

He tried to work out where he might head next, how he might be able to find Auch'ray's home. Surely Flucknor wouldn't have left him where he had done if the path forwards hadn't been obvious.

Or did Flucknor have something else in mind for him?

Lou's mind spiralled back to those conspiracy theories, the ones that just wouldn't seem to go away, and he found them hard to shake. After all, supposedly, Ravensbark, all those monks there, were Hildie's friends.

And then he thought back to Damon's expression when he'd told him about her burning those villages to the ground, and he knew that either Damon was a terrific actor, or he'd been unable to conceal his disgust . . . or confusion, whatever he'd felt about hearing of Hildie's actions. Even though Damon had been the one to joke about it first.

Another shudder ripped through him and he decided that he really didn't care about the politics being played here, about whether or not he might be being used as a pawn in a much larger game.

What he cared about now was finding some warmth. Else he might die up here, freeze into a block of ice up on this mountain ledge. Unless his ice magic saw fit to save him.

He watched his breath form steam before his eyes, and hang in the air in its hot cloud. He reached down and felt for the Webbing Blade. Touching its handle helped a little, served to bring the cold around him into context, with its own burning chill. He felt his heart stirring in his chest, and, just over his shoulder, he heard a distinct clicking sound.

For some reason, the first place that Lou thought to look was back at the rock, behind him. Back to that sable-tone of rock which gave its name to the Sable Mountains. There was nothing there, though, of course.

He studied the clicking sound a little harder. It seemed to be coming from all around him, from all sides. His mind flurried with possibilities. Could it be some new enemy? A magical beast, perhaps?

He'd heard that they all hid out here in the Sable Mountains, where the Kingdom of Shellacnass had exiled them to, left them on the point of extinction . . . or so they had learned in school.

He remembered Flucknor mentioning the magical beasts in passing, and he'd almost discounted it out of hand, because he knew that the notion of a magical beast was totally ridiculous.

And yet, standing out here, listening to that relentless *click-click-click* forced him to rethink his preconception.

It was funny what a little wind and ice and darkness could do.

Finally, and Lou wasn't certain how the idea sprang into his mind, he thought to look up, over his head. He studied the gloom there, tried to peel back the fog with his gaze.

Was there movement?

Could he see something descending towards him?

He squinted to try and see better, and soon drew the conclusion that, yes, there was certainly something descending towards him. Apparently on the end of a rope.

Click. Click. Click.

A mechanism, that was what it was. Lou could hear it whirring too, now. And he kept on staring above him, watching the descending object enter the glare which the torches beside him gave off.

A basket.

That was what it was.

A large basket.

It swayed in the gusts of wind, battering against the rock face as it descended, and, a couple of times, twirling round on the end of its line, of the rope which it was being lowered with.

Only as it came within a head and shoulders of him did Lou think to step aside for the basket to drop those final few feet to the ground. He watched it ease itself down onto the mountain ledge, down onto the pit-black rock, just inches from his toes.

The basket came to a halt with a slight *rustle*, as its wicker made contact with the stone.

Lou waited there, his breath hitched at the back of his throat. He gazed up, once again, although he could see nothing but gloom riding over him. He hoped to see the person in charge of the basket's winch, but it was impossible.

And so, looking round him, still feeling extremely uneasy about being out here, standing in the middle of the Sable Mountains, hail tumbling all round him and wind gusting from all directions, he clambered over the side of the basket and landed inside.

He stumbled as he landed, but soon found his footing. And he waited, wondering what was going to happen next. Then, perhaps drawing on something someone had told him long ago, or thinking back to some story his ma or pa had re-laid to him, he tugged a couple of times on the frayed rope.

It remained taut, holding the basket upright.

A slight pause and then the basket lurched upwards.

Lou momentarily lost his footing, but snatched hold of the side of the basket before he took a tumble. And it was a good thing too seeing as the basket veered sharply over to one side, showing him a little too much of the ground for his liking. The sight inspired Lou to hold on all the more tightly, to burrow his fingernails into the wicker.

As he rose he felt the hail strike him again, come raining down on him. He summoned up the courage to flip the hood of his cloak up over his head once more, to cover himself from the worst of the barrage.

And then, finding standing a little problematic what with the howling wind gusting over the basket, he dropped down and made himself snug in the base of the basket.

Even through the fierce chill of the wind, and the rattle of the hail, the most overwhelming aspect of the basket was that stink of wicker—somewhere between the smell of wood and freshly bound hay.

He got hit with twin reminiscences, of his pa's carpentry, and being back out there, in the fields, bringing in the yield on Midsummer's Day. As he was struck with the nostalgia, and perhaps to take his mind off the basket as it swung about, twirling on the end of its rope, crashing into the rock face over and over again, he wondered whether he preferred his life before or after the fire that had done for Endmere. Before he had joined the skullers. Before he had had the nerve to show so much as doubt in Herbert Junth's leadership.

Because, as he often reminded himself, most things aside, he had got himself into this position all by himself.

And it would be up to him to adapt to the situation.

Or die.

The basket climbed higher and higher, and Lou felt his stomach take several tumbles. Although he would never admit as much, he had never been one for heights, and being blown from one side to the other in this basket did nothing for that fear.

And so he reached for the Webbing Blade once more, and curled his fingers around its handle, and felt its ice magic soothe him, as if it nibbled at the ice magic within his own veins.

The *click-click* of the mechanism continued unabated, and Lou caught another bout of ice on his tongue as he breathed in. He was sure he could hear the mechanism winching the basket upwards, working harder now, getting louder. And he knew that soon he would be at his destination.

Wherever that was.

He gripped tight to the handle of the Webbing Blade as he rose, and felt the basket come to rest, still dangling precariously in mid-air.

Another torch stood posted into the mountain. And it provided a healthy glow about his current location, shedding off light in all directions, always seeming to be only another whisper of wind from being blown out altogether.

But the wind never quite managed it.

The wind buffeted the basket from both sides, blowing it hard against the rock face, and then out many feet from the tip of the mountain. The mechanism was in sight now, a simple wooden wheel with the rope wound about it. And no one there to operate it.

From his position at the base of the basket, Lou eyed the gap, knowing he would have to bide his time.

And jump.

He prepared himself, allowed his hand to leave the handle of the Webbing Blade, and he caught the rhythm of the wind. He waited it out. Felt it gust hard against his cheeks, and chill him to the bone. It dropped. And then picked up again.

And then, once more, the wind dropped.

Lou jumped.

Lou felt as if time had drawn to a halt all around him. It was like he was in mid-air for what seemed like an age. He had enough time to blink several times, for his heart to rap seemingly a thousand beats, and for his stomach to take a dozen or more rolls.

And then, before he knew it, the mountain was beneath him. Beneath the soles of his boots. And he felt his knees buckle as he landed there on the icy rock.

For a gut-wrenching moment, he felt the soles of his boots slip off the icy surface, and his heart beat back up to his throat. But somehow, perhaps with the aid of another gust of wind from the opposite direction, he regained his balance and stood his ground.

He glanced around him, taking in his surroundings.

He stood on a thin—a *razor* thin—mountain edge.

There was barely enough room for the mechanism which had lugged the basket up the rock face, and even less room for explanation of what exactly had powered that mechanism.

Or what kept the torch lit when exposed to such a fierce gust.

But, as the wind blew in once more, Lou saw, using the torchlight, that there was only one real possible way to head along the mountain edge, and that was to keep setting one foot in front of the other. One way along the edge seemed to become narrower, while the other way got wider.

And Lou had enough sense about him to know which he should choose.

He kept his cloak wrapped tight about him, snug to his chest, and he stumbled his way along the edge, no longer afraid to look down, because, on both sides, there was only blackness.

And certain doom.

Lou kept on moving along the edge of the mountain. When he noticed the ground beneath his feet begin to widen, the rock becoming more accommodating, he realised that he had been so certain that he was going to die that he let loose a mighty gush of laughter.

Which the howling wind soon carried away.

He trudged onwards, now seeing another glow, out of the gloom, opening up before him. He had a direction to head for, and so that was where he went. He stumbled onwards, feeling more blind now than he had at any other stage of this journey.

And yet he knew that he had to keep going.

If he wished to be an ice mage then this was the path he must tread.

But that did nothing to ease his fears as his boots knocked pebbles tumbling off over the cliff edges and into the ever-lasting darkness at either side of him.

He never even heard those pebbles clatter when they reached the bottom.

The torches grew stronger still, so much so that he could now make out forms in the half-light, and yet he wasn't sure whether or not to trust them. If it might just be his brain making things up, trying to keep him from madness.

But Lou was sure.

Up ahead, he could see it. A topsy-turvy cottage, built out of sturdy wood, with a thatched roof, apparently unmoved by either the howling gales or the pounding hail.

In fact, it was almost like there was a protective charm bestowed upon it.

Yes, he could see that slight, iridescent sheen now, could see it glowing against the torchlight.

And he was certain that he had found his destination.

Lou's heart pounded against his tonsils as he took the final steps up towards the cottage. And then he found he could go no further. He had come up against the protective charm.

He ran his fingers along it, remembering when he'd practised casting one himself with Hildie, and how, by way of demonstration, she'd cast one herself, and allowed him to touch it from the outside.

But this protective charm, it was nothing like Hildie's had been.

Whereas Hildie's charm had felt like it had something of the resilience of a bubble off a wash bucket filled with soap, this charm felt like smooth glass. He could run his fingers along it, almost hear a mournful note come off it as his fingertips came into contact.

This, Lou knew, even despite his fairly minimal, and extremely practical magical education so far, was magic on a level that he had thus far never experienced.

Another gust of wind blew along the mountaintop, and he felt it creep round the collar of his cloak. He narrowed his eyes and tried to calculate his way into the protective charm, into that cottage that sat smugly inside.

He could see the gentle, slightly orange glow coming from the windows, and, as he turned his attention to the roof of the cottage, he saw the ramshackle, stone chimney smoking away. Its smoke passing through the protective charm with, apparently, no obstacle.

If only he could turn himself to smoke.

But, even if he'd had the knowledge, he wasn't a fire mage.

Perhaps, with training and time, he might be able to turn himself to fog. There was little point in hoping about that now, though. Now was the time for practicalities. He had to think about how he was going to get inside as little more than Lou the Working Hand.

Lou prowled the perimeter of the protective charm twice trying to find a way inside. The cottage occupied this entire flattened mountaintop with, what seemed to be, in the near darkness which sprung up at either side of the sheer drops, no more than a few paces clearance on any chosen side.

He knew that a landslide might spell disaster for the cottage situated up here on this mountaintop as it was. Although, and Lou had a strong feeling, if this really was the home of Auch'ray, and if half the things which Hildie had sprouted about him were somewhere near correct, then he supposed there was very little chance of the cottage toppling over the edge any time soon.

When Lou got back to the front of the protective charm, to where he could look to the front door of the cottage, he decided that while he might not be able to dismantle the protective charm completely, then at least he might be able to burrow his way through a small portion of it.

Because that was all he needed, wasn't it?

He just needed to get himself inside there.

Finally, to safety.

And so, he reached down to his side once more, and felt for the handle of the Webbing Blade. He drew it from its sheath, and held as firmly as he could in his trembling hand. He decided that, what with his miniscule repertoire of any kind of specific ice magic, he might as well just take what might've been called, in his former occupation, the agricultural approach.

He clasped the handle of the dagger tight and then thrust it hard at the protective charm.

As he stuck the blade in hard, hard into the protective charm, he felt an uncontrollable shudder seize hold of all the nerves in his arm. But the blade was going through, it was making its way through the protective charm, he could see it happening.

And rather than the feeling of breaking through glass that he had half-expected, the effect was more like, as he knew from experience, plunging the blade into a human chest.

He felt it tear at the protective charm, and, before he allowed himself to forget his task, he made a square shape in the charm, carved it out of thin air.

His muscles all bunched up and his nerves caught fire as he worked hard to make himself a doorway in the protective charm, a hole big enough to fit his whole frame through.

And, through the never-ending sheets of hail, and the roaring wind blowing his cloak all over the place, he bundled in through the gap he had created.

Inside the protective charm.

18

IN THE HOME OF A MASTER

LOU FELT HIMSELF TINGLE all over. It was that sensation he had come to realise as the proliferance of ice magic ripping through his bloodstream. He knew that he had exerted himself, that he had drawn on a large amount of magic using the Webbing Blade as his conduit. But now he had achieved his task.

He had broken through the protective charm.

As he lay there on, what he soon found to be, the grassy lawn before the cottage, he stared back at the hole he'd made in the protective charm, watched it seal itself up, much as a well-watered hole collapsed in on itself. Soon the hole was indistinguishable. Completely invisible. And he knew that, at the same time as he was safe, he was also trapped.

He ran his tongue over his teeth, still not quite able to believe that all the chattering of teeth he'd done on his journey had failed to crack any enamel and, finding that nothing showed up following this superficial check, he moved onto considering himself for any broken bones.

His muscles were sore . . . well, some of them were crying out in sizzling pain, but when he eased himself up, back up onto his feet, neither of his legs gave way. And when he replaced the Webbing Blade back in its sheath, his arm seemed perfectly fine.

His nose, he was pleased to note, felt much better now. Although maybe it was just numbed by the freezing winds he'd endured to reach this point.

He listened hard, to the wind howling outside, and to the hail pattering off the protective charm. It sounded like ice on glass, even though Lou knew that the protective charm was merely magical matter, and the only thing that kept the elements away from the very much exposed cottage here.

He glanced to the front door of the cottage, took in its fertile green colour, and then, looking around, realised how well it reflected the garden.

Auch'ray, for Lou was now sure that was who lived here, kept roses, spiralling their way up a trellis on the outside of his cottage. And there were hedgerows. And neatly hoed flowerbeds, with flowers that Lou would never even attempt to name.

He wondered how many of these flowers carried magical properties.

Then again, why else would a great mage such as Auch'ray keep a garden unless it had some practical purpose?

Lou found the garden path, which consisted of a series of hefty, pit-black slabs, all embedded in the lush lawn. As he made his way along it, he felt the sturdiness of the rock, and felt the sharp tang of the flowers' scents clambering up his nostrils.

And he felt the hairs stand up on his arms as he approached the door.

And then he waited.

And waited.

He felt frozen, but this time not from the cold.

Now he was frozen by fear.

And expectation.

Even after this long and arduous journey he felt like nothing more than an imposter. An imposter who'd shown up on a stranger's doorstep and who expected hospitality.

As Lou drew back his fist to knock, the door opened in on itself. A rush of heat billowed out onto his exposed cheeks, like a warm embrace welcoming him inside. And yet, he held back, because, in the doorway, there was no one.

It appeared that the door had opened on its own.

He ran his tongue over his lower set of teeth, feeling the ridges there, still trying to eek the numbness out of his mouth from the climb up here, and he caught the scent of a hearty broth weave its way through the air from the inside of the cottage.

And that was probably what got the better of Lou's manners, as he took the decision to step over the large hearthstone and enter the cottage.

Next, Lou heard the crackling of flames, and it sounded so out of place, considering his long and hard trudge to get up here, that he could barely believe it was real. In fact, he wouldn't have believed it real if he hadn't seen the smoke coiling up out of the chimney outside.

He turned and looked about him, trying to take in the cottage at once, attempting to locate his host, so that he might apologise for arriving up here, on this mountaintop, and breaking through a protective charm, uninvited.

But there was no one in sight for him to ask his apology.

The sturdy wooden beams stood out from the cottage walls, and from the roof over Lou's head. The plaster was a sallow shade and obviously several decades, if not centuries, old. And the whole place reeked of the broth, the broth that, looking about the room, Lou couldn't locate.

He turned to look behind him. There was a set of stairs which spiralled upwards, and then, to the side of the stairs, still on the ground floor . . . or as much of this first level of this cottage up on this *mountaintop* could be described as *ground* . . . he saw another doorway.

The only one leading out of this room, other than the front door he'd just come through.

And, as Lou turned his head in the direction of that doorway, he breathed in that meaty goodness, and the buttery-sweet edge to it, and he was almost certain he could hear it bubbling away, somewhere in the distance of the cottage.

He guessed that to be the kitchen.

He waited for several seconds and then, deciding that he'd gone on long enough, standing here in a stranger's house without announcing himself, he said, "Uh, excuse me?"

He listened for an answer, but heard nothing by way of reply.

He felt a lump form in his throat, and his gut started to grumble away, surely inflamed by the prospect of that meaty-broth smell burrowing its way through the air of the cottage.

"Hello? Is there anyone here?"

No reply, yet again.

He took a step along the floor, hearing the wooden floorboards creak beneath his feet. A shiver ran up his spine, as if he was a burglar, looking to snatch whatever he could from this cottage.

A burglar who had just climbed a mountain to do so.

Anyway, looking round this room, he saw that there was really nothing *to* steal. And not that he was a burglar at all. His parents had taught him well on that lesson, or perhaps it had been the sight of seeing a man from outside the village, from outside his hometown of Endmere, get caught stealing a shank of meat. And lose his right hand for his trouble.

He took another step forward. Another creak from the floorboards beneath him. The scent of the broth got richer in the air, and made the back of his mouth water. He reached down to his side, and rested his fingers over the handle of the Webbing Blade.

Its chilly waves pattered through his chest and went some way to calming his hunger pangs.

"Uh, hello?" Lou said, now walking at a normal step, heading for the kitchen.

No response this time either.

He reached the doorway to the kitchen and looked in on the place.

It was fairly basic, although he had little idea of just what he'd expected to find here, up in this cottage tottering on a mountaintop.

There was an oven, standing off to one side, and an open fire blazing beside it, on which Lou saw the large metal pot bubbling over the flames. And the scent of the broth just became overwhelming. Right now Lou could hardly believe that last night, that even *this morning*, he had felt so completely full from the feast that he'd thought it no trouble to fast for a month.

That had been before he'd climbed a mountain.

Before he'd broken through a protective charm, and a *good* one at that.

He glanced about him, spending a long time on the shadows of the kitchen, trying to scope out whether the owner of the cottage was playing a trick on him.

But he found no one.

He looked to the boiling pot of broth and then, looking to its side, he noticed something crackling from inside the oven. He waited where he was, in the doorway of the kitchen, just a few seconds longer, and then he shifted back, looked back in on the sitting room, to the front door of the cottage.

"Hello?" Lou said, feeling the hunger pangs making his voice whiny, uneven.

Again, nothing.

He heart swelled up in his chest, and he felt his gut pulsing with hunger pangs now. He simply had to get his hands on some of that nourishing broth. Just a bowlful. That'd get him back to his full strength.

And so he returned to the kitchen, sidled up to the boiling pot, and, finding a pile of bowls standing beside the pot, he snatched one off the top and dunked it into the simmering broth, taking care not to burn his fingers.

He brought the bowl up, and watched the steam cascade off its surface, and that sweet, buttery smell just . . . *somehow* . . . grow all the sweeter.

His hunger was too strong for him to bother looking about for a spoon and so he set his lips to the cusp of the bowl and drank, long and deep. And, of course, once he'd drained it, that bowl was nowhere near enough. So he took another helping. And then another.

After his third, he thought a fourth serving would be imprudent.

But he took it anyway.

And then his curiosity got the better of him and he knew that he simply must take a look at just what was baking away in the oven.

He stooped over it, feeling the broth still thick in his mouth, and still warm on his lips, and he unlatched the door to the lower section.

He glanced inside, and saw a pair of bread loaves baking away there. Side by side. Nestled together looking just as delicious to Lou like a pair of pigs fattening up to slaughter.

Well, there were two bread loaves, who was going to miss *one* of them?

And so, reaching inside, and almost instantly feeling the heat become unbearable, but equally not daring to withdraw his hand, he slipped out one of the bread loaves.

As it turned out, the bread itself was about the same temperature as the oven, and so Lou had to shift it from hand to hand, feeling his fingers burning, and letting out miniscule little groans as he did so.

Finally he thought to let the bread drop onto the stove, at the top of the oven. He kicked the oven door shut with his foot, glad not to feel the baking heat through the leather of his boots, and then he feasted on it.

Only when he'd finished the bread, and had *another* serving of the broth, did he hear the door to the cottage creak open on its hinges. And Lou's heart welled in his throat.

He looked to the soiled bowl, and then to the breadcrumbs scattered all about him, sticking to his shirt, and he knew that this was no way for him to have made an impression.

Or not a *good* one, in any case.

Lou fixed his gaze onto the doorway to the kitchen, listening to the front door closing, slamming shut, and the sounds of the tinkling hail on the protective charm outside fade. And then he listened to the inevitable footsteps beating their way across the floorboards of the sitting room.

He could picture the man in his mind now. Cheeks rose-red, lips puffed out and an irrepressible anger in his eye. Furious. And why shouldn't he be? Lou couldn't blame him.

And so, when the footsteps grew louder still, and then a figure darkened the doorway, Lou was completely taken by surprise to note that the man was smiling. He was grinning right at Lou.

"Louson Dorf!" the man said, with a merry rise to the tone of his voice.

Lou felt a tingle run through his bloodstream, and his heart knock down on his stomach. He could already feel the broth taking him over from the inside, warming him up.

Now he had time to take in the man's appearance. He looked about seventy, or eighty summers old, and he had a bushy white beard which seemed of one part with the rest of his thick, equally white hair.

The man was spry, spindly, and although hunched over, clearly a little taller than Lou.

Auch'ray?

The man bundled across the kitchen, towards Lou, and, just for a second, Lou was certain that the man might be about to change expression at any second, that he might draw a dagger from some unseen location and jab it into Lou's stomach.

It would've been so easy for the man to dispose of the body since all he would've been required to do would've been to drag it out to the mountain's edge and give it a nudge with his foot.

But the man didn't draw a weapon at all, and he didn't check his pace either as he rushed right into Lou, throwing his arms round him in an embrace the strength of which Lou had never felt off even the strongest of his uncles.

In fact, he felt the air near enough being thrust from his lungs.

When the man was finished, he loosened his grip on Lou, but still clutched his tunic in his fingers, and he stared Lou in the eye. Lou saw that he had brilliant, almost star-blue eyes. And that those eyes still had that unmistakable youthful sheen to them. A sheen that could never be defeated, not even with a lifetime of winters.

"Louson Dorf," the man repeated, and then his smile cracked even wider, if that was even possible. "Yes, I've been expecting you. Hildie told me to expect you."

Lou still felt struck dumb, and a little frazzled by the whole encounter. And then he remembered his manners and, managing to shuck the man's clutches for a second, he glanced back to the blazing open fire, to the pot of broth still boiling away there . . . though it was only about a quarter full now.

"I, uh, I . . ."

The man caught his eye, and then looked over to the pot. His eyes widened. And then he turned back to Lou, still smiling. He clapped Lou on the shoulder and chuckled. "Ah, good, I'm glad that the journey's done nothing to defeat your appetite, my lad." He gave Lou another clap on the shoulder, and then stalked off to the oven door, which he cracked open and glanced inside. "And the bread, too, my goodness!"

Lou didn't quite know what to say, how to read this man. He wanted to apologise, but the man didn't seem to be in the slightest inclined to giving Lou the window of opportunity to present one.

The man tutted to himself as he peered closer to the oven.

"Just one loaf, though." He glanced back over his shoulder to Lou. "Didn't have the stomach for another?"

And then, as if on cue, Lou's stomach grumbled, long and loud, distinguishable even against the loud crackling of the opening fire, and the bubbling of the broth in the pot.

The man cackled out.

A laugh that made Lou feel more than a little uneasy.

The man shook his head as he backed up from the oven, and then, with a flick of the wrist, slammed the door shut. He rested one hand on his hip and, with the other, scratched his balding scalp, eyes half-closed. "Now," he said, "if only I could remember where I'd left the preserves."

"The preserves?" Lou managed, finally finding his voice.

"Yes," the man said, still scratching his head, and then, as if struck by a lightning bolt of realisation, he glanced back over the kitchen, to the doorway, where Lou saw the man had dropped a cloth sack there, which he must've done when he'd rushed across the room to embrace Lou.

The man snapped his fingers and went to retrieve the sack. He brought it up in his hands, and fumbled with the drawstring, and then he opened it up to reveal several jars, all sealed tight, within the bag. There must've been half a dozen. He pawed through them, checking the labels written out in a hand that Lou simply couldn't decipher, and then he tapped his finger at the one which, apparently, he'd chosen.

He grinned again at Lou. "Been out gathering this afternoon, before the storm set in. Only just got myself back now. Never like to be out there in the night, but sometimes the weather can be unpredictable up here in the Sables, eh?"

Lou supposed this was the point where he was supposed to agree, despite being a long way off being an experienced campaigner of the Sable Mountain. "Uh, yes," he said, somewhat unconvincingly.

The man clasped tight to the lid of one of the jam jars, and unscrewed it. And then he glanced back at Lou. "Go on then, aintcha gonna take a seat over at the table over there, with that other bread loaf?" He turned his attention back to the jam jar. "Terrific stuff, this, warm you right up, get all your senses pounding again, it will."

Lou suddenly felt feeling restored to him, and he picked out the table in the corner of the kitchen, over by the window, looking out into the lush garden, and then to the somewhat surreal scene of the hail stones bouncing off the invisible protective charm.

He shifted his feet and took up his place on the wooden bench, even remembering to bring the remaining, still-warm, bread loaf along with him. And he sat down there, feeling the hardness of the wood beneath his bottom, and finally allowed the tension to ebb out of him.

Lou thought about what Damon Shriversmyth, Abbot of Ravensbark had said about Auch'ray, about how he was a 'moody' bastard, as he'd put it. And Lou couldn't help thinking—unless he'd somehow got the wrong house—how far of the mark that description of Auch'ray's character really was.

19

THE FIRST DAY OF TRAINING

T HE NEXT MORNING, Lou stood out on the mountaintop. The snow and hail had cleared, and a pristine blue sky spread out over the Sable Mountains. He could still taste that jam he'd smeared over his bread from the previous night.

He had never *ever* tasted anything quite like it.

Thinking about it, he compared it to hazelnuts, something he'd tried once when a vendor had passed through Endmere. Yes, hazelnuts combined with blackberries.

Auch'ray, because it did turn out that was his name, that Lou had found the right place, explained that the jellied substance grew naturally a little further out, in a high-grass plain nestled up on top of a hill.

He informed Lou that it was seen as a delicacy, and that it was really quite valuable in the Kingdom of Shellacnass. Lou took his word for it, because, right now, standing up here on this mountaintop, he had very little consideration for making money, for scraping together a few grung, and all the concentration for the Webbing Bow, the grip of which he held tight in his hand.

He glanced off to Auch'ray, saw the still-grinning mage watching him from several paces away, spread back on his lawn, clearly enjoying the mountain air and the sunshine beating down on him.

Soon after Lou had finished his jam-smothered bread the night before, Auch'ray had shown him upstairs, to the upper floor of the cottage . . . which was to say, *one* of the upper floors of the cottage. Because, as Lou had soon realised upon climbing the stairs, the floors just seemed to stretch on and on, upwards and upwards without coming to an end.

And, after they'd levelled out on one of those floors, Auch'ray had shown Lou to a room in which a bow hung off a wall.

The Webbing Bow.

Lou thought back to how he'd taken it in, to how the Webbing Blade had felt down at his thigh. He'd quite distinctly felt the ice magic rip through it, almost burning against his leg. Much stronger than anything he'd ever felt before.

The Webbing Bow itself had just as ragged appearance as the Webbing Blade, and Lou knew this to be because of its age, that it was a magical artefact that had been passed down through the years, through the *millennia*, and so it had passed through the hands of so many mages on its way.

When Lou had pressed Auch'ray for the names of the mages, perhaps hoping to hear some stories that might help out his own case, he had been greeted with the first frosty silence between them. But even that hadn't lasted too long, as Auch'ray had bounced forwards and snatched the Webbing Bow off its bracket on the wall, held it out for Lou to take in his own hands.

Lou remembered that first curl of cold heat that had passed

over his hands, and still the stirring of the Webbing Blade in its sheath. He had almost dropped the Webbing Bow right away, and he could still recall the slight twinkle in Auch'ray's eye as he'd watched him take hold of it.

That look had reminded Lou of something, there had been something more to it. Perhaps even a *fatherly* aspect to it.

And Lou had drawn back the string, given it a few practice lashes, and felt it whip against his unguarded forearm. That chilly pain had been a lesson, a lesson that he'd learned right from the start with the Webbing Blade.

That he *had* to respect the magical artefacts he held in his hands.

Lou felt the cool morning, mountain breeze blowing against his cheeks, and he could smell that long grass hanging there, seeming to strip away all the weariness he felt inside himself, to ease the knotted muscles within his body.

Being out here, *up* here, on the mountaintop, it seemed to have a knack of restoring him totally, to bringing back his strength of mind as well as his strength of body. And Lou knew that he'd need all that he could get of both.

He reached back for the quiver, still feeling unfamiliar having it over his shoulder, and he took hold of the tail of one of the arrows and, keeping his hands steady, notched it into the bow, just the way that Auch'ray had taught him.

Lou felt Auch'ray's eyes on him, from his position lying back on the grass, and he knew that although the man looked quite relaxed, picking at the sweet blades of grass, he was watching intently, keen to seek out the potential which lay within Lou.

And Lou was determined not to disappoint him.

Lou gripped the bow tight, feeling the wood creak beneath his hold, and he drew the arrow back in the string. When he reached the tautest point, he felt the elastic nature of the string almost quivering beneath his touch. And he felt all the pent-up force there, ready to be spent.

But, more than anything else, he felt Auch'ray's eyes burrowing into his skin.

He could feel that ice magic bypass his skin and penetrate his bones, chilling him utterly.

Lou breathed in, and then let loose an exhale, and then, breathing in again, he let the bow string go, and the arrow slipped past his other hand.

And planted itself into the earth, a step or two before him.

Lou sighed long and hard, feeling his shoulders rise and fall with his frustration. He'd been at this ever since the sun had risen, had fired off . . . if *fired* could even be the right word . . . in the region of fifty arrows. And all of them, without exception, had burrowed right into the earth at his feet.

Actually, looking at where he'd fired the arrow now, he saw that it had got a good couple of hairs' breadths from the others.

Progress, of a kind.

Lou glanced to Auch'ray who still lay on his side, staring into mid-air and kneading his beard through his thumb and forefinger, apparently thinking. Lou guessed that he could afford breaking Auch'ray's train of thought. The situation kind of demanded it.

"What now?" Lou said.

Auch'ray blinked a couple of times, and slowly met Lou's eye, as if he'd been rudely woken from a dream. "Hmm?"

Lou allowed the Webbing Bow to fall down to his thigh, to where it hung just inches away from the Webbing Blade. He felt that familiar icy throb pass between the two weapons, as if they were wolves, on a whited landscape, howling out to one another for comfort.

"I can't do it," Lou said. "I've tried and tried. I told you that I'm no good with bows . . . I couldn't use crossbows even. The only thing that I can partially manage is a sword."

"Or daggers," Auch'ray said, nodding to the Webbing Blade sheathed at Lou's hip, and grinning from ear to ear. Then he snapped back onto Lou's gaze. "You've just got to remember what I've taught you, about how to aim, about how to stand. You'll get there eventually."

Lou let loose yet another sigh, perhaps completing a baker's dozen for the morning, if not more, and he whipped out another arrow, set it again in the notch, and went through all the motions, doing everything Auch'ray had instructed him to do.

He pulled back, breathed in, and then out, and then in again, and—

"Wait!" Auch'ray called out, still not shifting from his spot of the lawn. "Remember what I said, as you let loose you must breathe *out*, okay? Got it?"

Lou grumbled something, and then, taking note of what Auch'ray had said, he released the string just as he breathed out.

And the arrow flew far.

Further, at least, than the previous arrow.

Which was to say it embedded itself a pace or two further along.

Lou worked at his bow-and-arrow skills long into the twilight and then, as the cool, clear night sky opened up above him, and the stars all came out twinkling, he practised some more.

He had made some progress now. At least he'd reached the stage where, with a fair amount of the time, he could fire his arrows off the mountain ledge, and into the abyss. He almost never tired of that feeling, of watching the arrow duck and weave through the air before plunging off, and being lost forever.

As he let loose his latest volley, he watched the arrow ping through the air and then out of sight, losing its trail in the mounting darkness.

He turned on his heel and looked to Auch'ray, who was standing now, wearing a cloak, and staring off in the direction of the disappeared arrow. When he turned back, to face Lou, he was still smiling, but Lou noticed that something of the sparkle had gone from his eye.

Lou knew that he'd let the man down, that he'd had high hopes for him. It had been enough just to take in how the man had acted towards him, that fatherly feeling Lou had put his finger on earlier. And now the man saw just what he had to deal with.

Lou felt for another arrow from the quiver. His hand wandered back over his shoulder, feeling for that giveaway tickle of the arrow's tail. But he couldn't find it no matter how hard he tried. And yet, he'd been sure, just before he'd fired off that last arrow into oblivion, that he'd felt several there. Certainly five or six of them, if not more.

Out of the corner of his eye, he noticed Auch'ray trudging towards him, his face just as grim as Lou's performance deserved. Lou busied himself with the Webbing Bow in his hands, looking down at it, secretly glad that this seemed like it would be the end to the day's training session.

To the day's humiliation.

He pressed his lips hard together and waited for Auch'ray's encouraging voice, but with the disappointed tone burrowed away there, not so unsubtly hidden below the surface.

Auch'ray's sure grip found Lou's shoulder, taking hold of him again, and giving it a squeeze.

That same *fatherly* squeeze.

"Good work," Auch'ray said. "You've done well today, considering just where you started from."

Lou stared off into the darkness, almost scathing himself to visualise that arrow, where it was perhaps still descending, barrelling downwards, and deeper into the unknown regions of the Sable Mountains.

Unknown to him, in any case.

This time, though, Lou couldn't restrain himself. He bunched himself up, shrugged off Auch'ray's hold, and then swore beneath his breath. With the Webbing Bow still tight in his hands, he stormed off across the garden, and over to the edge of the mountaintop, where he stared over, into those layers upon layers of darkness.

He listened for the soft footsteps of Auch'ray pursuing him over the lawn, but there was no sound. And up here, standing right on the edge of the mountaintop, Lou could smell the ice in the air, that irrepressibly fresh tingle that wormed its way right down his throat.

Which almost froze his tongue.

But cleared his senses.

He waited there, staring down and down, and playing out the day again through his mind. He had just been impossibly bad, irretrievably bad, and he'd made a mockery of everything. He *was* an imposter simply being up here, having come to seek Auch'ray and have him train him. The only thing Lou had succeeded in doing was wasting both their time. It was obvious already that Lou would never be a mage, that he would never be anything more than a working hand . . . and perhaps if he worked hard at that he might have a chance of one day being a landowner. But *mage*? It was enough to make him laugh.

And yet, it made him want to cry.

Lou still waited for those soft footsteps, that almost inaudible brush of grass against Auch'ray's bare feet, and his gentle breathing, that unshakable smile of his. And that bitter, *bitter* disappointment.

But there was no sound of Auch'ray's approach.

Feeling the chill of the moonlight wash over his skin, seeming to ignite further the ice magic in his veins, Lou glanced back over his shoulder.

Auch'ray wasn't there.

Lou looked to the cottage, to its still-smoking chimney, and then to the glow from the windows, that woozy orange glow from inside. He hadn't even heard Auch'ray take a step across the garden. He thought back to what Hildie had said, about the best mark of an ice mage being his invisibility, being able to move with the shadows, his ability to simply slip into the wind, into the darkness.

But that was never anything which Lou would achieve. Not in this lifetime at least.

He stared away from the cottage, back along the edge of the mountain, to the basket and the winch that led to the way back down the rock face, and away from Auch'ray.

Was that what Auch'ray expected him to do? Had he been examined and been found wanting, and now expected to, quietly, and politely, take his leave?

Lou considered the journey back. At least he had Ravensbark

to look forwards to, to rediscovering Flucknor's company. That was something at least.

If they'd let him past the front door.

But then he thought about the journey itself, and how he'd have to make it on foot, he would have no horse to fall back on, to carry him the whole way there.

He looked up above him again, tasted that ice on the wind, the wind that had surely carried the ice off some unseen mountaintop, drifted it right over here, to him. And he felt that same ice magic stir in his veins, and he looked down to the Webbing Bow still clutched in his fist.

How was this supposed to work? Should he lay the Webbing Bow down at the front door of Auch'ray's cottage . . . the Webbing Blade too? That might be expected.

And then he cast his mind back to the encampments, to the villagers that depended on him, to what Hildie had said, about him being able to go back there to protect those people . . . *his* people. Without the Webbing Blade what was he?

He wasn't any more than a mortal with a bit of magic in his veins, that was the truth.

He couldn't protect *anyone* as Lou the Working Hand.

But as Louson Dorf the Ice Mage, he might have a fair chance.

He looked back to the cottage, and to the snug interior that awaited inside, and then, without so much as another glance back along the mountain edge, to the basket which would commence the way back down the mountain, head for the path back to Ravensbark, he padded softly along the grass to the front door of the cottage.

20

THE LEGEND OF THE SPIDER WARRIOR

LOU BROUGHT THE DOOR SHUT with a firm, and decisive, *slap*. He felt the cold from the outside air chill him round the collar of his tunic for a few moments, and then felt it cast off in the face of the reassuring warmth of the sitting room of Auch'ray's cottage.

The moment only lasted a moment, though. Because, soon enough, as whenever he drew close to fire these days, he felt that familiar prickle of the ice in his blood. As if it was thawing.

He could smell that same broth cooking up, and he could also smell that jam: that mixture of blackberries and hazelnuts in the air. And he only had to cast his glance to the corner of the sitting room, to the open fire which Auch'ray had apparently lit in the fireplace there, to see Auch'ray himself, sitting in his armchair and contemplating the flames.

He sat with his fingers steepled, and his eyeballs swiftly moving over the flames, as if scoping out his advantage over an old enemy. And, Lou considered, *fire* was his enemy.

The enemy of them both.

Lou could smell the ash in the air, and he could sense how it burned at the base of his lungs, and sent the ice in his blood flurrying through his veins.

A log on the fire crackled hard, and this seemed to be the signal to Auch'ray to turn his head towards Lou, and say, "Do you know why I live up here, on the top of the mountain?"

Lou felt his chest tighten, and was glad that the first word past Auch'ray's lips hadn't been asking him why he hadn't gone off, why he hadn't left for Ravensbark, to go back where he needed to be . . . where his real place in the world was.

Lou shook his head in answer to the question.

Auch'ray smiled faintly and then gazed back into the flames. "Because," he said, "it is a constant reminder of the value of that which can destroy us." His eyes reflected the firelight. "And which can also keep us alive, which we *need* to keep us alive. You see, we have to live with fire, that's the way of the world, even *us* . . ."

Lou sensed how Auch'ray lingered over the 'us,' and Lou felt the word sting his veins just as potently as any ice magic.

". . . we need the fire to stop us from dying," Auch'ray finished.

Lou stared into the flames too, and he couldn't help thinking about Hildie, about what she might be doing right at that moment, if she'd truly kept her promise to him, to protect the encampments while he was gone.

And then his mind returned to that kiss.

It lingered for a long while over that kiss.

Lou clutched the Webbing Bow tighter still, and waited for Auch'ray to speak again, when he did his voice was gravelly and ragged, and none of the earlier jubilation, the constant enthusiasm which had seeped through his voice before, was there.

"I must tell you," Auch'ray said, "and it must be early in our relationship, so that there be no sort of misunderstanding." He glanced back over his shoulder, looked Lou right in the eye. "What have you heard about me?"

Lou felt his chest open up, and the ice burn all the harder through his veins. It felt like someone had chopped up glass and set it into his bloodstream. He thought back to Damon Shriversmyth's saying that Auch'ray was a 'moody bastard,' but that couldn't be what Auch'ray was getting at, could it?

And so he said, in a quiet voice, hardly rising above the crackling of the wood on the fire, "I knew nothing."

Auch'ray mumbled something, a vague gargle at the back of his throat, and then spoke louder so Lou could hear. "Do you know of the existence of the Magical Council?"

Lou thought back to his lessons with Hildie, to her rapid-fire dictates on the ways of the magical world, and how she'd brushed over various aspects of the place. But . . . a Magical Council, yes, he'd heard her mention that. And then it came back to him in that moment, he realised that was where Ma'reygar had gone . . . to petition other mages to join him in the forthcoming magical-mortal war.

That was what Hildie had told him.

"Yes," Lou replied, feeling his voice quiver.

"Hmm," Auch'ray said, and then gazed back into the flames flickering before him, and he dangled his arm down the side of his chair, his fingers flexing and unflexing as he did so. Without turning away from the flames, he continued, "Do you know *why* they don't allow me onto the Magical Council?"

Lou thought about this for a moment. He had speculated, from where Auch'ray chose to keep his home, far away from everybody, and with the slightly eccentric picture he'd built up from the various pieces of gossip about his character from different people, that Auch'ray would merely never be *inclined* to join such a council.

He *liked* to be alone and divided from the rest of them.

"Well?" Auch'ray said, this time with steel in his voice, still staring into the flames, and Lou could only focus in on the fluffy white hair which stroked the back of his neck, like cotton.

"No," Lou said.

Auch'ray stirred slightly in his armchair, and from the way he sucked in air from the fireplace, and his face seemed to twitch in profile, Lou knew he was making his master uncomfortable. But when Lou opened his mouth to speak, to excuse himself, and leave Auch'ray to one of his apparently 'moody' moods, Auch'ray spoke again.

"It's time you heard of the Spider Warrior, are you familiar with that at least?"

Lou thought long and hard on that, and he admitted to himself that the name sounded familiar, and then he recalled Hildie telling him about the legend . . . back in Ilsnare, had it been? So much had happened in the space of a few months that already his memory was failing him.

Lou nodded and then, realising that Auch'ray was turned away from him, he parted his lips to speak again, but Auch'ray had seemed to acknowledge, if not *see* his nod, and he continued to speak, still staring—*always* staring—into the flames.

"The Spider Warrior is what you are already two thirds of the way to becoming."

Hearing that, even though, from what he'd gathered from Hildie, he knew to be true. She had told him about the three magical artefacts which made up the Spider Warrior's armoury: the Webbing Blade, the Webbing Bow, and the Webbing Cloak. He only needed the Cloak now to complete the set . . . assuming that he would *ever* become proficient enough with the Webbing Bow to allow himself to even begin mastering the Cloak ...

... whatever mysteries the Cloak held in store.

"Yes," Auch'ray said, "I cannot believe that Hildie would have failed to tell you about the Spider Warrior, if she told you nothing more."

Auch'ray shifted in his seat, straightened his back, like a cat waking from a nap, and Lou was certain that he was on the cusp of turning round, of looking Lou in the eye. But, no, Auch'ray just kept his back to him.

"Before you," Auch'ray said, "I had another apprentice. A boy by the name of Xeda. He was from some town in the Sable Mountains, the name of which I do not remember, because it was destroyed a long while ago." He drew breath, and Lou was certain he saw a shudder pass up his spine.

He knew that a shudder passed up his own.

Auch'ray continued, "He came to me, much like you, although he had yet to acquire any of the magical artefacts, let alone had he already taken two into his possession." He sighed, long and hard, and Lou watched on as the flames flattened out momentarily before sprouting upright once again. "No, when I met with Xeda I was certain of the ice magic in his blood, much stronger than any I had ever encounter, any that I have *yet* to encounter."

Lou felt his gut stir a little. It took him a second or so to identify the feeling. Jealousy? Was jealous from the implication of Auch'ray's statement, that Lou couldn't be a better prospect than Xeda had been?

"But also," Auch'ray continued, the skin round his eyes wrinkling, "I saw more than just an apprentice." He paused for a long while and, again, the only sound which filled the sitting room was the crackling of the flames, the gentle *snaps* as the bark burned off the wood. "I saw an *opportunity*."

Lou stood there, rooted to the spot, staring after Auch'ray, waiting for him to continue. What did he mean by opportunity? He cast his mind over the thought, and about how that was just how he had viewed Hildie seeing him. She saw him as an *opportunity*, a chance for her to get some mortal bodies involved with her magical war: some pawns held up for sacrifice.

Auch'ray stayed where he was, in his chair, still staring into the flames, impossibly still now. Lou caught the reflection of the flames in the glassy surface of his eyes, and he was almost certain he could see black clouds moving beneath the surface of his eyes, of the thoughts and memories all bouncing around there.

Or it might've just been a trick of the light.

"Yes," Auch'ray said, "what I saw was an opportunity. A glorious and once-in-a-lifetime opportunity, because, you see, I had just happened across the locations, or the approximate locations of all these magical artefacts: of the Webbing Blade, the Bow, and the Cloak."

Lou remained stuck in silence, almost able to feel the weight of the words thickening in the air, and he waited for Auch'ray to continue. He stalked a step closer. And, almost as if in response to the story that Auch'ray was telling, he could feel the Webbing Bow twitch in his grasp, and the Webbing Blade cool at his thigh.

Auch'ray shook his head. "And so I took the boy on, I took Xeda on, and I taught him all I could, of the light, and the dark, of the fire, and the ice. I helped him to improve his charms, although already I could see that his own potential *far* outstripped mine. I knew that, on a level playing field, in a matter of a few years, I would be nothing more than a bug beneath his boot to him." He breathed in a snappy breath. "If his own power didn't devour him first."

Lou could feel the chill off the Webbing Bow getting strong, and seeming to swill, to join up with the influence of the Webbing Blade, to rift through the air. And, without thinking, he set the Webbing Bow down, at his feet, and slipped the Webbing Blade from its sheath.

This story was enough to take in without the magical artefacts playing havoc with his senses.

Auch'ray continued, "And so I got him as far as he would go"— he paused momentarily, as if to correct himself—"I got him as far as *I* felt comfortable taking him, because I didn't want him to find his own true potential before time, and to perhaps challenge my own authority. No, I wanted him strong . . . but only strong enough.

"And when I chose the right day, the right time, I instructed him on the three magical artefacts, the three most powerful weapons in any ice mage's arsenal. And, what was more, I told him just where to get them from."

For the first time in what seemed an age, Auch'ray turned in his chair and looked over at Lou, and Lou felt the weight of his gaze on him, and he could see that Auch'ray's eyes weren't *glassy*.

No, he was weeping.

Auch'ray continued, "Of course, Xeda, being extremely ambitious, and wanting to please me, his master, he swept off without question, clutching the map which I had passed onto him." He sat very still, eyes still drifting over Lou, and his focus seeming to ebb in and out. "And that was the last I knew of him."

Lou felt a surge in his chest, and his blood coil up through his veins, towards his heart. And he couldn't help blurting out, "What?"

Auch'ray smiled faintly. "Yes, the last I heard of him until I heard of the Spider Warrior: the undefeatable ice mage who was rampaging across the land." Auch'ray's lips parted, and Lou watched the silent tears dribble their way down his cheeks. "By then, of course, it was far too late for *me* to do anything, even as the second most powerful mage in the land, I would have no hope against him. Xeda had spent years in the wilderness, honing his skills, skulking away in the darkness. There was simply no hope, or so I thought."

Lou waited for a long time. One of the logs on the fire let loose a sharp *hiss*, and then broke up in a series of crackles and crunches. He watched it collapse into ash in the fireplace, and watched the dim orange embers burn away there.

"And then what happened?" Lou said, now past the point of caring what pain this inflicted on Auch'ray, because he knew that he had to finish the story, that Lou *had* to know what had happened to the Spider Warrior.

"Another," Auch'ray said, "another came along. The strongest fire mage in the land . . ."

And even before Auch'ray spoke the name, Lou knew just what he was going to say.

. . . "Ma'reygar."

Auch'ray shook his head and lowered his chin down onto his chest, the tears still flowing freely and, Lou saw, his hands shaking as if gripped by an invisible tremor. "Ma'reygar, if it hadn't been for him then we might live in a very different world—a *totally*

different world. All I heard was from travellers as they'd pass through the village in which I was living. This was a different time, when mages were tolerated throughout the land, and even celebrated in their villages. But the Spider Warrior changed all that.

"When they saw what pure, unchecked magic could do to a land, tear the whole place up, *murder* women and children in their beds, then the mortals could no longer tolerate it. And they exiled all mages from the land, imprisoned them where they could, tortured or killed them when they got the chance.

"Ma'reygar, though, when he managed to defeat the Spider Warrior, to burn him to death, he inherited the three magical artefacts. Of course, then, there was no discussion about who should take the High Chair on the Magical Council, Ma'reygar was voted to take the position and he accepted quite willingly.

"However," Auch'ray's words seemed to stick in his throat for a moment or so, they seemed to become obstacles to him, "after only the first matter to be voted on came to pass, Ma'reygar's position as High Chair of the Magical Council was immediately struck into doubt."

"Why?" Lou said, feeling his chest stick, and his heart hammer on harder.

"Well," Auch'ray said, "the issue rested on who was most worthy to possess the magical artefacts, and several possibilities were laid out. The first: that they should pass to an appropriate ice mage on the Council, and that they should be put into great care. Of course, Ma'reygar was obstinate about that possibility, seeing as it would've meant passing a great power onto an adversary, as Ma'reygar has always seen all other mages." He paused for a long while and then added, "Even his daughter."

That mention of Hildie sent another tremble through Lou's gut, but he tried to push her face from his mind's eye. He had to concentrate. He had to learn. He must see just what Hildie had told him the truth about, and which truths she'd chosen to omit.

"Another possibility was raised, that the magical artefacts should be scattered about the land, in hard to reach places, as they had been before, so that no one would be able to get a hold of them without great strife, and only a great mage, one stronger even than Ma'reygar would be able to obtain them."

Lou felt his eyes rounding, and the breath sticking in his mouth. He could feel hunger pangs again trembling through his stomach, but he shoved them down. Just didn't care at all. He had to know. "And where were the magical artefacts spread to?"

"It was agreed by the Council that it would be the ideal situation to have only one mage know about the locations of the artefacts, and also to be better if the mage who knew of the locations was *not* on the Council."

"You?" Lou said.

Auch'ray inclined his head, in faint approximation of a nod, almost so subtle as to imperceptible. "And so, I resigned my post on the Council, although I had no doubt it would've been stripped from me if I hadn't offered it so readily."

"And so how did the Webbing Blade end up in Ma'reygar's hands?"

Auch'ray let loose a long-held sigh, and Lou saw that the tears had stopped, and that a new weariness had entered the old man's eye. And now, despite all his spritely activity, his rushing about and seemingly boundless energy, he saw the fatigue ebbing not so deeply beneath the surface.

"I gave it to him," Auch'ray said.

"What?"

Auch'ray nodded. "Yes, he had ideas, plans, Ma'reygar, he had ideas of how he might combine fire and ice magic, that he might be able to create a new hybrid, to join the two types together and become some *all-out* master of the magical world. And it seems that he succeeded, in casting that curse which hangs over Ilsnare, the Crystal City, the one which turns the animals feral, and which seems impossible to shift, even to my eye."

Again Lou felt that fresh stirring within him, the embers of anger in his belly, and the heat rushing through his blood. He could almost taste his own blood in his mouth, laced with ash and ruin.

"I suppose I saw it as a kind of recompense for Ma'reygar having defeated the Spider Warrior, it seemed only natural that I pass the weapon to him." He glanced down at Lou's feet, to the bow which lay there. "The Webbing Bow stayed with me, came to my new home here, up on this mountaintop, because surely it would take a real mage to climb a summit to reach it, isn't that so?"

Lou felt a fresh thrill through his chest, knowing that *this time* Ma'reygar was referring to him. But he shoved it to one side, knowing he had to focus. "And the Webbing Cloak?"

That sparkly-eyed smile returned to Auch'ray, the one which Lou had almost believed to be lost forever as he'd wept through this story of the Spider Warrior. "Ah," Auch'ray said, "that can wait until a little later."

Lou stared into the lowered embers in the fire place. He could still feel the waves of heat coming off the warmed bricks. And he could still smell the ash in the air, and how it combatted him from the inside, made the ice in his veins skitter and swill.

He was taken off guard a little when Auch'ray spoke again, because he had been almost certain that he'd used up all his words for the evening, that he'd expended all his emotional reserves.

But it appeared that there was still energy for one thing.

A little word.

"Another reason I live up here, on the mountaintop," Auch'ray said, "is because this is the place where the sun's rays are strongest, so as an ice mage I not only walk in strength, I walk in weakness too. And that is something which must be borne in mind by any aspiring mage." He paused for a second or so. "For *any* mage at all."

Lou thought on that, thought about how he'd been so concentrated on working out how he might get stronger, how he might become more at one with his powers, get himself up to the level which might see him acknowledged as an ice mage, that he really hadn't considered weakness at all.

But that would change.

It *had* to change.

21

LONG DAYS TRAINING

LOU WORKED HARD every day with Auch'ray, getting up before dawn, and then working throughout the day on his archery skills, before, in the evenings, having sessions to improve his charm casting.

Once Auch'ray invited Lou out into the middle of a storm, hail hammering down on them, perhaps about the same level of intensity as the storm on the day Lou had arrived.

Lou recalled strongly the rattle as the hail fell, the few windowpanes it smashed in the cottage, and the sting as those hailstones—falling just as hard and fast as *actual* stones—pinged off his cloak.

And then Auch'ray had shown Lou how to cast the protective charm, the one which Lou had broken through by using the Webbing Blade. And he'd stood in awe for a long time, at first struck by the scale of it as much by its consistent strength. When Auch'ray invited Lou to cast his own, Lou could only smile at the suggestion and refuse.

Auch'ray let him off that night, telling him that since he'd already cast the protective charm it would be a waste of Lou's energy in any case. But, Auch'ray said, with a slight lilt to his voice, he *would* have Lou practise casting his protective charm at some point.

If he ever wanted to become an ice mage he must.

Lou didn't think to mention that he *had* succeeded in casting a protective charm, back when he'd rescued Sully and Rut, but it seemed long ago now, and almost relegated to the edge of his mind, that he doubted if it had really happened at all.

Neither did he mention anything further about the Spider Warrior . . . about Xeda . . . and it seemed that Auch'ray was equally glad not to raise the topic of his own accord.

Lou had everything he needed to know right now—didn't he? —and so he was much better off looking to the future, looking to see what was laid out before him.

Auch'ray also told Lou more about the Magical Council, about how there were seven fully-fledged members, and how they took all the decisions regarding magical policy throughout the world.

Lou made a point to repeat the names of the members of the Magical Council to himself as he lay beneath his blankets in bed at night—those warm, lambswool blankets—and stared up into the starry sky outside his window. He recited each name in his head, as Auch'ray had instructed him:

Ems'plot: Ice.

Kwar: Fire.

Lumbswich: Ice.

Grendlin: Fire.

J'plaut: Ice.

Wyd'rswen: Fire.

And, finally, Yunt'ga'boar: Ice, and current High Chair of the

Magical Council, although, from the way that Auch'ray spoke about him, Lou got the impression that he didn't trust him at all.

Despite him being from the same class of magic.

Auch'ray also instructed Lou on the nature of the balance of the Magical Council, about how the institution was constructed so that one type of magic would have prominence over the others for a time ... until it was seen as being time for change.

And Lou asked after Ma'reygar, wanted to know whether or not the Council were likely to approve his call to arms, for them to start an all-out magical war, and Auch'ray responded that it would all depend on which way the Council would vote.

If they could really see provocation from the mortal side being reason enough for war.

But, from the way that Auch'ray's words slithered off at the end of sentences, he knew that, to Auch'ray's mind at least, he could see the world only heading in one direction.

Lou now saw that his role in this world wasn't to attempt to evade war, to try and help someone to finish the prospect of war, but his responsibility was to his people, to all those refugees back at the encampments. His duty was to protect them, to shield them, from all this chest-beating between the mortal and magical realms.

One evening, the both of them sat before the fire. Lou felt the ice magic prick against his veins, protesting about being so close to the flame—that had been one of the consequences, or benefits, of his increased training, of getting more in touch with his magic, now whenever he walked in the sun or got close to fire he felt himself hurt from the inside.

Like he was bleeding away inside of himself.

But he sat there all the same, ignoring his body's protests. He wanted to be an ice mage, and if he wished to achieve that dream then he would have to overcome pain and weakness . . . *no*, like Auch'ray said, he would have to embrace it.

He could taste the remnants of the broth he'd suckled down only an hour or so ago, and he could smell the ash and smoke from the fire crawling its way up his nostrils. And he could hear the slight stir of the logs in the fire, the harsh breathing of Auch'ray as he dozed, eyelids half closed, chin resting on his fist, staring into the flames.

Lou knew that he had to ask, and he had to ask right now. He might not get a better opportunity.

He turned his head towards Auch'ray and said, "Are you trying to make me into another Spider Warrior?"

For a few seconds, Auch'ray remained in his same daze, as if he was intently listening to something the fire had to say to him, or as if he could see something in the flames that was beyond Lou, or at least beyond Lou's vision. And then he snapped out of it, blinked away the daze, and his eyes lolled onto Lou. "You know the story, and I believe that we know each other well enough now, from our time training together, not to tell one another lies—not to try and deceive one another."

Lou waited, feeling the warmth from the fire become almost unbearable now, seeming to cause his heart to bulge up in his chest, and threaten to burst right through his ribs.

Auch'ray continued, "So that is why I ask you to believe me when I tell you that my only role is to show you your true potential. Please, believe me, I have no stake in a magical war." He let loose a catlike yawn, then stoppered it with his palm. "I'm an old man, Louson, and I'm not interested in shaking up the kingdom for whatever reason. I'm happy up here in my home, nestled on this mountaintop, out of everyone's way. We've already seen what a nuisance I can make of myself in this world. So it's better for everything this way."

Lou thought about what he'd said, and about the destruction the Spider Warrior had wreaked throughout the kingdom, how he'd slaughtered mortals, and become the subject of night terrors.

Corrupted by his power.

"So," Lou said, "what're you saying exactly?"

"Just what I've already said, that I want you to see your true potential, from my angle, from where I sit in all this posturing, I really have no interest to what end you serve that potential."

Lou curled his fingers into fists, digging his fingernails into his palm and feeling the sting of his fingernails cutting into his skin. He sunk his teeth into his lower lip too, just trying to bear the blaze of the fire against him, causing all the ice magic inside to foam up and threaten to burst right out of his veins.

Now was the time. Just as he was sure that Auch'ray had been honest with him, it was time for him to be honest with Auch'ray, to lay things out clearly for both of them to see.

He looked to the old man, releasing his skin from his hold, and his lower lip from his teeth. "Hildie, she told me to come here. She expects me to lead my people . . . to have them form an *army* to fight against Herimyre, and the Kingdom of Shellacnass, to lead a *siege* on Ilsnare."

Auch'ray took this information with a wry smile, and a slight twinkle in his eye, but otherwise he stayed silent.

"And," Lou continued, "she wants me to take a hold of these magical artefacts, to collect them all together, so that I might fight on her side. Lead her to victory over the others."

Auch'ray nodded along, now fixing a sombre frown on his lips.

"She wants me to be another Spider Warrior, and she wants to *use* me."

Auch'ray stayed still for several moments, and then removed his chin from his fist, where he was resting it, and he straightened up in his armchair. He opened his eyes wide, and Lou thought he was about to yawn again, perhaps thinking of excusing himself from this discussion on the pretence of going to bed, when he spoke once more.

"Are you quite sure?" Auch'ray said.

Lou thought long and hard, about how Hildie had sworn to protect the encampments while he was gone, about how she seemed to be fixated on everything to do with the brewing magical war, and not to have any attention left over for resettling Lou's people, to having them rebuild homes. And he was certain.

He nodded in reply to Auch'ray's question.

"Very well," Auch'ray said, with a slight pout, "and have you considered the option of refusing her?"

"Of course, that's what I intend to do."

"Then why're you puzzling over this? What are you hoping to achieve?"

"I just wanted you to know—wanted to be honest with you."

Auch'ray shrugged. "I have no allegiance with Hildie, or her father, and I don't pretend to either. They're friends, *good* friends, I suppose, as far as that goes. But all that falls to me, as an elderly mage, is to instruct you to the best of my ability, to pass on my skillset to the next generation. To pass on my secrets. What you do with them is up to you."

Lou breathed in hard again, and he felt the smoke from the fire billow round his lungs, and take away his senses for a moment. He thought to the Webbing Blade and the Webbing Bow nestled up in his bedroom, and of the Webbing Cloak . . . out there *somewhere* in the world, just ready for him to find it.

That was his duty.

To his people.

And he was determined that when he returned to the encampments, he would be twice the mage that Hildie was, and he would be able to easily defeat her.

Thinking about that kiss between them, back on the bridge leading across the valley to the Sable Mountains, now it turned him sick to the stomach, just to even picture it in his mind, to think of those soft lips pressed up against his own.

A trick, that was all it had been.

Just a trick to make him trust her.

And, in that instant, he felt the pang of realisation pass through him, and, now knowing that Hildie was not to be trusted, he knew that he had to be back at the encampments as soon as possible. That he couldn't afford to leave his people with her for too long.

She would turn them against him.

Perhaps she was trying to make herself a leader.

He knew her strategy now, that she had seen him as a vague threat and sent him away, up here, into the mountains, on a fool's errand, and meanwhile she would take on the mantle, and begin the process to lead the people of the encampments back to Ilsnare, to fight against the Royal Guards.

And, most likely, to die.

Lou turned his attention back to Auch'ray, almost certain that he had been listening in to his thoughts, following his exact logical process and that, even as he stared into those flames, apparently lost among them, he had concluded just the same thing.

Lou felt the words weighing down his tongue, and he knew that the time had come, the time for him to say goodbye. But, before he could, Auch'ray broke in and said, "This war, this war that Hildie has it in her mind to wage against Ilsnare, it's simply impossible. Simply with my ear to the ground, hearing all the developments up here, in the Sable Mountains, hearing the gossip which floats my way from the Magical Council, I know that it's far too late. That this war cannot be prevented."

He pressed his tongue into his lower lip for a moment and then continued, "All that it will mean is more death—more *mortal* deaths, and I'm sure that even Hildie shall see that it's in vain.

"Young Louson, you've done well with me, and it joys me to say that you've learned quickly and well. Now that I've taught you everything that should build a foundation on your path to becoming a full ice mage, you must make your own decisions." He paused for a second, and then said, "I must tell you of the location of the Webbing Cloak." He paused again, a slight rasping sound entering his breathing. "But, not quite yet."

Lou knew this not to be the truth, that he still had so much to learn from Auch'ray, and that he could teach him, but, at the same time, he sensed that Auch'ray understood the predicament that Lou found himself wrapped up with. And that Lou simply *had* to follow his own path, and return to help his people.

And as for the Webbing Cloak, well, for the time being, he hoped he would get by just fine with the Webbing Blade and the Webbing Bow. He could start thinking about completing his armoury, about starting down that same road as the damned Spider Warrior, once he'd got Hildie away from his people, and he'd lead them to safety from all this madness.

THE FINAL MORNING IN THE
MOUNTAINTOP COTTAGE

LOU PASSED a sleepless night beneath his impossibly soft lambswool blanket. He could still feel the remnants of the fire permeating the whole cottage, and making his skin tingle, and glow, all over. He could still taste that wonderful nectar, the jam that Auch'ray had introduced him to, the one which stripped away his hunger and fatigue and thirst. When he breathed in, though, all he tasted was ash.

And he knew that it was from the simple thought of Hildie.

He waited till the sun had risen to just the cusp of the mountaintop before shucking his blanket and placing a foot out of his bed, onto the wicker rug which lay on the wooden floor. The wicker rug made a slight creaking sound beneath the weight of his feet.

He dressed quickly, putting on his cloak, the Webbing Blade, and then the still-unfamiliar burden of the Webbing Bow, and the quiver full of arrows which accompanied it.

Although he wasn't about to win gold in any archery competition any time soon, he had promised himself that he would keep on practising, and that he would get better as time went along. When he arrived back at the encampments, he would take every spare opportunity to practise his aim.

Fully-prepared, he padded down the stairs, and into the kitchen, already warmed with the smells of breakfast cooking, and already occupied by Auch'ray standing at the stove, and pawing through some scrambled eggs.

Lou often wondered if Auch'ray kept animals nearby, or if there was some village just over the next cliff face that he hadn't had the chance to see during his stay at the cottage.

The two of them ate through their breakfast in silence, although Lou caught Auch'ray several times glancing over his own breakfast plate in Lou's direction. One of the times Lou managed to meet his gaze, and though Auch'ray kept up his slight frown for the first few seconds, he soon cracked that all-too-familiar smile.

He now knew Damon Shriversmyth's character description to be totally inaccurate. Sure, Auch'ray, up here, away from everyone else was isolated, but that didn't mean he wasn't kindly or caring or warm . . . despite the ice magic which flowed through his veins.

In fact, the more that Lou thought of it, he came to the conclusion that Damon, and *not* Auch'ray, was the 'moody bastard' between the two.

Lou could still recall the frosty reception he'd got back at Ravensbark, and wasn't likely to forget that for some time.

As Lou sipped at his tea, he thought that the monks were something that he hadn't yet had the chance to ask Auch'ray about and so, deciding this might be his final opportunity before he left . . . and who knew when Lou would be back? . . . he decided to step in and get it out right away.

After asking the question, a simple one of wanting to know

what the monks' place within the magical community was, Auch'ray chomped away on his toast, and Lou noted the trace of egg yolk caught in his white beard. But he said nothing, just concentrating on the old man's words.

"The monks, eh?" Auch'ray said. "Yes, the monks, that is a good question. What purpose do they serve us, as mages, as members of the magical community?" He chewed up the last of his toast, swallowed it down, and that familiar gleam returned to his eye. "The monks . . ."

Lou waited for him to elaborate, but Auch'ray seemed all of a sudden lost in thought, just like Lou had noticed over the last few weeks, about how his concentration would somehow dip in and out of a conversation, as if his mind got all fogged up by some memory or other . . . or by something which Lou couldn't see for himself.

Auch'ray continued, "The monks serve as a type of magical equilibrium, they fall to neither side of the spectrum." He held up his thumb and forefinger of both hands and, inverting one of his hands, created a square with the fingers. "Imagine a diamond," he said. "And then think of the four classes of magic, the four *moods*, for want of a better phrase. They all occupy one of the angles of this diamond, one of the corners. We have ice and fire as opposites in this diamond, and then light and dark, too, another pair of corners, also opposites."

Lou stared at the diamond Auch'ray had created with his fingers, and imagined to himself the fire and ice in a pair of opposing corners, while darkness and light were at the other pair of opposing corners. This made enough sense to him . . . so far.

"Now," Auch'ray said, "the monks, they sit right in the middle of all this. They are neither light nor dark, neither fire nor ice. They sit right here in the centre of our diamond." He studied Lou through the diamond, and Lou guessed he was trying to see if he was paying attention to this, if he was absorbing the basics of what he was saying.

Sure, Lou might've been a working hand, but he thought he could at least grasp this. When he got it all diagrammed out and explained in a condescending manner, that was . . .

"The monks are a sort of magical standpoint, they show us degrees of magic around them, and it's up to them to preserve their magical purity, which is why, no doubt when you went to Ravensbark, the Abbot there was rather short with you, didn't go out of his way to make you feel welcome at all."

Lou guessed that was one way of putting it.

"That is because the whole of the magical community trusts in the monks keeping themselves apart from any of the corners of this diamond of the magical balance of the world, and if they were to align themselves in some way we would lose that reference point, and chaos would ensue in the magical world. They must take extreme caution in who and what forces they allow inside the walls of Ravensbark, the whole magical world depends on it."

Now Lou felt his annoyance with the Abbot start to ease a little. Although he'd heard something of this off Flucknor, it was another matter entirely getting it explained to him by an ice mage of Auch'ray's standing. Whereas he might've interpreted Flucknor's remarks earlier as some way of apologising for his boss, out here, on this mountaintop, with someone who had no stake in his relationship with the Abbot . . . well, it made it a bit easier to comprehend.

Auch'ray paused, as if considering whether or not to continue. Finally, he unlinked his forefinger and thumb, and lowered his hands down onto the table. Then he said, "What happened with the Spider Warrior, what happened to Xeda, was that he strayed too far over to the *ice* side of the spectrum, and it ate him up, and split him in two, corrupted him inside and out.

"Now, the mark of the true mage, the one who can have true and lasting success in the magical and mortal realm, is the one who can stay neutral, remain, somehow towards that centre point, not lose himself in either fire or ice."

"And what happens then?"

"Well," Auch'ray said, "what happens then is that, if he continues to better his craft, strives to be the best mage he can be, while staying neutral, he ends up as either a light or dark hero."

"And which are you?" Lou said.

Auch'ray grinned again, long and hard, and then, slowly, muscle by muscle, the smile slackened from his cheeks. "I gave up wanting to be either hero a long time ago, and that's also why I live up here. My whole life revolves around staying neutral, on not straying too far towards any corners of that diamond: not fire, or ice, or light or dark. That's my life now."

"And what do you recommend I do?"

"Well now," Auch'ray said, sticking his tongue firmly into his cheek, "that'd be for you to decide for yourself."

23

ANOTHER PROTECTIVE CHARM

OUTSIDE THE COTTAGE, up on the exposed mountaintop, the clouds were forming above them. Lou stared at the ragged clouds, all dark-bottomed and stirring about, rolling over each other. They reminded him of paintings he'd seen of the sea, back in Endmere, when hobblesmen would stop by to sell their works.

He could recall one painting in particular, with a sky just like the one forming overhead, a deeply grey darkness dimming the whole scene, and the sea all choppy, white horses, as they were called, rolling back and forth.

When he'd asked the hobblesman the price, and the hobblesman had told him, Lou had almost staggered backwards, and fallen right down into the gutter of sewage that ran through the town square—where the exhibition of the artwork had been taking place.

Later on, he'd watched on, in the fading evening light as the hobblesman had packed up his paintings, slid them all into his cart, which he wheeled along behind himself, and then observed him roll out of town, taking the painting with him.

If only Lou had had the money he would've bought that painting in an instant, if he hadn't needed to save every last grung for the hard winter ahead—because there was *always* a hard winter ahead—he would've indulged himself.

Perhaps later, when he became a successful mage . . . *if* he became a successful mage, then perhaps he would be able to seek out another hobblesman, another with a painting of the sea just like the one he had seen, and buy it from him.

Or, just perhaps, Lou might get to see the sea for himself.

That would be a fine thing too.

Auch'ray tilted his head back as he wandered over the threshold, and out of his cottage. Lou examined the reflection of the greying sky in the glassy surface of his eyes, and he thought about how accustomed the man must be to the storms, since he lived amongst them.

As Auch'ray glanced back at Lou, that familiar smile tracing his lips, he listened to just what he had to say, what came from that dried-up old throat of his master. "Looks like a storm's rolling in," Auch'ray said.

Over the weeks Lou had grown accustomed to the obvious statements that Auch'ray would often utter. And this was no different from any of them. He'd long ago learned to discard these without any extra thought, not to bother himself with scouring them for some obscure wisdom.

He had grown to know that this part of Auch'ray's talking was coming from the old man part of him, the old *mortal* part of him. And Lou knew that, one day or another, maybe sooner than he anticipated, the man's great mind would be lost forever.

At least that would be in keeping with all the other old folks he'd known in his life.

"Yup," Lou said, casting a glance over the darkening clouds, all bunching up together, and he could already taste the rain in the air, could feel the ice on the wind, and smell the damp seeming to rise up from the earth beneath his feet.

In the distance there was a peal of thunder.

A shudder tickled Lou's spine.

Auch'ray slowly moved his gaze from the clouds above, bringing it down to take in Lou before him. And Lou felt the ice magic stirring in his veins, and a throbbing commence in his temples. He knew that he would miss his master but, at the same time, he would also feel a touch relieved.

Because he knew that, if Auch'ray chose to do so, he could crush him with his little finger.

That magical power, for Lou, would remain a mystery for a long time yet, Lou knew it.

Auch'ray's smile slipped from his lips, and a new steel flashed over his eyes. Lou felt his heart hammer against his ribs, and his breath come short and sharp in his lungs. But he didn't dare look away from his master. This was like Damon Shriversmyth had hinted at, all the 'moody bastard' seeming to rise back to the surface.

Lou got a strange and unshakable thought, that Auch'ray might be about to issue him an ultimatum, that he might be about to demand that he stay behind here, on the mountaintop with him forever, or that he might simply have decided he'd made a great mistake . . .

. . . and choose to destroy Lou right here.

Where he stood.

Lou felt the blood rushing to his gut now, and he felt for the shimmer of ice magic from the Webbing Blade and the Webbing Bow. The two magical artefacts seemed to be creating a great invisible capsule around him, enveloping him in their influence. He felt the shrill ice magic bring the hairs on his exposed arms up into a standing position, and he could almost feel the frost forming on his tongue.

But he stood his ground, knowing that any resistance would be futile.

If Auch'ray chose it, he could kill Lou with or without the Webbing Blade and the Webbing Bow.

Auch'ray was too powerful, too knowing of all four corners of the magical fields, of that diamond as he had illustrated it to Lou, not to be in complete control of any ensuing conflict.

When Auch'ray spoke, his features were just as grey, just as gloomy and ominous as the clouds forming over their heads, of the storm brewing up, getting ready to strike the Sable Mountains. "You must know about the Webbing Cloak," Auch'ray said. "But first I need to see that protective charm of yours."

Off in the distance Lou heard another peal of thunder and, suddenly, all around them, a blinding flash of lightning.

Lou stood still, feeling his heart hammering even harder up in his throat. And that field produced by the twin influence of the Webbing Blade and the Webbing Bow seemed to grow almost unbearable. He felt thousands of little pinpricks, all over the surface of his skin, and he traced how they moved, heading inevitably up towards his skull.

And, for the first time, Lou really understood what it was to be consumed by ice magic.

He resisted, muttered the charms which Auch'ray had taught him, the ones that would keep him safe, keep his body from being totally taken over. And, slowly and surely, he felt the pinpricks subside, and his consciousness come back to him.

A protective charm.

This wouldn't be too hard.

After all, he'd done this all before, hadn't he?

Lou met Auch'ray's gaze and saw that it was now completely devoid of softness, there was none of that personable, warm . . . almost *fatherly* look now. That was long gone. And somehow Lou knew that he was looking right into the soul, *deep* into the soul, of magic itself.

And a hollow and unloving place it was too.

Lou brought his mind back, and thought back to the time when he'd attempted to rescue Sully and Rut, it was so long ago now. And how he'd concentrated hard, and how those cursed crows had been bearing down on them. And how he'd saved them.

He *had* been able to do it.

Now, though, the situation was somewhat different. There wasn't any real peril for either Lou or Auch'ray, since he knew, at the back of his mind, that if Lou failed at his task, that if he failed to cast the protective charm before the storm broke, then Auch'ray would do so for him.

And *much* better.

But Lou had to try.

He had to show his master what he had learned.

That he was right to think of Lou as being a worthy apprentice.

And so Lou started to mutter the incantations, just as Auch'ray had taught him. Slight variations on the ones which he'd learned off Hildie, ones which would be a better fit for his own magical class. Just as Auch'ray had put it, Lou would only find the true extent of his strength by embracing his own ice magic, and working it into his light magic spells.

Such as this protective charm.

He felt himself hum, felt the blood inside of him begin to hum, and he got a weightless feeling, as if the toes of his boots were threatening to lift off the ground.

Somewhere off in the depths of his consciousness, he sensed a raindrop landing on his cloak, and seeping through to his skin. Another. And then another. Soon enough he could no longer count them as they fell.

And each raindrop brought with it an icy chill, and Lou felt it rattle him right down to the bone. But he kept up his muttering, those magical words, and concentrated everything he had down onto his solar plexus.

Everything slowed down, moved in minute detail. Just like he'd remembered back in the gaoler's cart, when he'd put his magic to use saving Sully and Rut. But now, now he was here, he could feel something different.

Whereas before he'd felt himself sheltered from all other sounds, that it was like he'd stepped inside an enormous protective shell, now everything came back to him just as loud as before.

He had no need to open his eyes to know that he had failed.

But he did so anyway.

As he took in his surroundings, he noted the skinny film of the protective charm he had cast. Or what would pass for a protective charm. The raindrops, though, ripped down through it with ease, and as for its size . . . well, it barely covered himself and Auch'ray, let alone the cottage off behind them.

Lou felt the icy raindrops splatter down, dampen his cloak, and turn his spirits sodden.

He just couldn't do it.

He knew he couldn't.

And, after a long, long pause out there, feeling the hail begin to form, and the raindrops replaced by the sting of ice, he looked over at Auch'ray.

Already, his master had his eyes closed, and he was murmuring his own form of the protective charm, the one which perfectly matched up to his own particular magical skillset. And Lou could only just about hear that murmur escaping his lips about the constant patter of the hailstones, landing all around them.

And then, with an extra chill to the air, Lou watched on as the glow emanated out of Auch'ray's own solar plexus, and lifted up from him, floating upwards, an effervescent cloud, a rare bright white light in the otherwise grey and doom-stricken landscape.

And he watched as it spread itself all over them, and expanded to encapsulate the whole mountaintop, with Auch'ray's cottage, much like Lou had seen it the first time, protected right in the centre of it all.

The hails stones stopped falling onto the pristine lawn, into the thick bushes or onto the rose petals, and they now hammered away at the top of the protective charm, rolling down like minute cannonballs to the base of the circumference.

The brief exasperation that Lou felt at having the hailstones off his back soon faded. Because he realised that he would *have* to step out there shortly. That he would have to leave behind the outstretched protective wing of his master and go his own way.

And through the storm.

Auch'ray's face remained stern, and his lips pressed firmly

together as he cocked his head to one side and regarded Lou. "You may stay another night if you wish."

Lou thought over the request for the briefest of moments, and then reminded himself of his people, of his suspicions that Hildie had betrayed all of them . . . that she'd betrayed *him*, and he knew, hailstorm or no, he had to set one foot in front of the other.

He *had* to return to the encampments.

That was his destiny.

And he had no need even to put his thoughts into words, because he knew that Auch'ray understood, that even if he could read Lou's thoughts, that wouldn't have been necessary.

Lou had his bag on his back, resting on top of the Webbing Bow, and he had the Webbing Blade down at his thigh, both weapons snug in their respective positions on his body.

He turned his back with no expectations, but Auch'ray still had a few words for him.

"The Webbing Cloak," Auch'ray said. "It's located in the Threaded Pit—the home of several mythical creatures . . . *spiders*. That is where you shall find it, if you can find the strength. *When* you believe yourself ready."

Lou thought this over, placed that in his mind.

The Threaded Pit.

So that was where the final part of his armoury was located, and he had no idea where that might be at all. And yet, he knew right now, standing there, having failed to produce the protective charm on demand, that he would *never* be ready.

He would forever be Lou the Working Hand, the great fakery that wished to pass as an ice mage.

But it was good to know, all the same.

24

HEADED BACK TO THE ENCAMPMENTS

LOU GOT HIMSELF back down the cliff face the same way he had come up it, in the basket. He watched on as the magical mechanism worked away, apparently indifferent to him. And soon enough he was back on the rocky floor, back on the mountain trail.

Ready to return to where he was required.

As he made his way along the mountain ledges, felt the hailstones pound down the path, skitter up all around him, he thought about whether or not he would return to Ravensbark, whether he could truly stretch his welcome to see how far it would go.

He decided against it, without much deliberation. By way of a parting gift, Auch'ray had given him a pot of the jam—the jam that tasted like a mixture of hazelnuts and blackberries—and so he would have almost infinite reserves of energy to draw upon, and so there would be no need for rest.

He would simply hike, day and night, to return to the encampments.

~

Lou supposed it to be around dawn by the time he felt his legs giving out beneath him and his heart jerking about in his chest. His legs felt like a pair of lead weights, dragging him back, threatening to hurl him off the edge of the mountain path and into the sure death of the valley below.

Even in the fledgling sunlight, in that pinkish glow, and with the clearing skies above his head, Lou felt that the river which ran the bed of the valley would be a welcome refreshment from his long and hard march.

He maneuvered his pack, the pack Auch'ray had given him, round to his front, and he pawed through it. He had already eaten his way through one jar of the jam, and he still had two of them remaining.

Although he had hoped to only eat one jar, two *maximum*, so that he might save at least two of them for later, for when he was back at the encampments and needed an extra degree of strength, but now he saw that most likely that he would need to consume all three jars.

If he was to arrive back at the encampments without first stopping off at Ravensbark.

Lou consumed half of the second jar of jam, and then headed on, already feeling the jam begin to work its magic, to restore his tired muscles, and the sores growing around his feet.

~

It took him until the late afternoon of his second day of travelling before he returned to Ravensbark. Not knowing the terrain at all, Lou had only had a gut feeling on when to expect it, when he would see it jutting out of the side of the mountain, its charcoal-black walls, so much like the wings of a raven its name implied. And so, when he did, it took him by surprise and he instinctively quickened his pace.

As he drew closer, he traced the mountain path which led up there, up to the stables, and he recognised it as the same trail he had travelled along with Flucknor. He had a strange longing, a simple *twitch*, inside of him that urged him to go back there, to visit the monks.

But his logical mind knew that he was not welcome, and all that Auch'ray had told him about the monks' position in the magical community, about how they provided balance to the world, was still very much present in Lou's mind.

And so, still eyeing Ravensbark, almost losing himself to those impossibly black walls, he ate through the last of his jam, and said a mental goodbye to Flucknor as he passed by, apparently without any reaction from inside the monastery itself.

Lou only realised he'd been heading downhill after several hours, with the sun already dipping down below the horizon, on his second day of travel. Only then, in the twilight, did he think to register that he was much, much closer to the river that snaked its way through the valley, through the Sable Mountains.

That he could hear its rushing torrents, its gushing streams, could feel its gentle, cooling spray carried on the wind.

While the jam, of which he'd now finished the second jar, and was thinking of commencing with the third, took care of his aching bones, and his stinging muscles . . . made him forget about the blisters that now lined both of his feet, it did nothing to soothe his mind, to make up for the lost nights of sleep.

And, so, simple lack of concentration was what he blamed for his predicament now.

However, at the back of his mind, he did feel that shred of his fantasy being fulfilled strike him, that wish of wanting to dip into this river, to feel its cool water lap over his skin, to strip away the sweat and dirt which clung to him, returned to him.

But he was in a hurry.

He *had* to get back to the encampments by tomorrow.

He was determined.

And yet, he could feel his mind torn and frayed, and his concentration dipping in and out. He walked along the dirt path, feeling the pebbles scatter from beneath his sozzled feet, and skitter off into the long grass at the side.

Although he told himself that he must turn round, that he must find another way, the *high* road, he felt the unshakable urge to simply keep going.

To just put one foot in front of the other and forget everything else.

And so that was what he did, and his feet carried him right to the banks of the river.

Before he knew consciously just what he was doing, he was crouching down, and then sitting. He was casting off the Webbing Bow and the Webbing Blade, laying them carefully down onto the dirt beside him. And then he was removing his boots, and his socks.

He felt the cool evening breeze brush against the raw skin at the soles of his feet, nibbling at those sores like a baby bird at a worm.

He held back for as long as he could, wanting to savour the sensation. And then he plunged his feet, one after the other, into the rushing stream, and he watched the crystal-clear, freezing, water lap over his tired feet, massaging them, restoring them, rubbing moisture into his leathery and strained skin.

And he closed his eyes, and felt himself floating away, as if his mind had simply detached itself from his skull, and was escaping him, rushing upwards like a puff of smoke from a wood-burning stove.

He felt sleep jabbing at his brain, squidging it about, and forcing itself on him. And he felt the moonlight licking against his exposed skin, against his face, and his neck, and his forearms, and he knew that he had to give in.

That he would have to wait until tomorrow to reach the encampments.

And he prayed that he wouldn't be too late.

25

ARRIVING BACK TO THE ENCAMPMENTS

A S IT TURNED OUT, the night's sleep did Lou's brain a
world of good. Although not quite enough not to necessi-
tate a hearty serving of jam on a piece of now-dry bread which
Auch'ray had given him. He munched his way through it, the *whole*
jar, at the bank of the river.

He watched as the currents of the river swilled and beat along,
constantly pressing harder and faster, never stopping to rest or
relax. He wished he might be more like the river. But that was just
a spiritual thought, something his ma might've said . . . when she'd
been alive.

Before Hildie had *murdered* her.

And that recollection, along with the tingling that passed
through every nerve in his body as he absorbed the bread and
revitalising jam, was enough to stir him into action. And it went
some way to pushing off the influence of the sunlight on his skin,
and its weakening of his every sense, and how it seemed too peel
him from his bones.

Now he would know what it was to walk with weakness.

He strapped on the Webbing Bow and the Webbing Blade once more, and he broke off his camp, doubling back on himself to continue his ascent of the mountain trail, and to get back on course to returning to the encampments before sundown that night.

Lou had no real conception of where he was, how far he had come through the Sable Mountains, until he started to recognise his surroundings. He had no idea what it was exactly, which *exact* detail told him just where he was, because, other than the day of his departure, he'd never passed along the trail leading to the Sable Mountains in his life.

But he *did* recognise it now, and then, just up ahead, he spotted the bridge, going over the valley. And, looking down, he saw the river running down there too, and he wondered whether it was the same stream that he had rested by the night before.

He liked to think it was.

At least one of its subsidiaries.

Lou beat the trail harder now, and he could feel all the aches and pains returning to him, along with the greater wish of his brain to take a much longer, a more profound, rest. And yet he found a new strength within himself now, because his whole body seemed to sense that he was almost back home . . .

. . . or, at least, the place that he called home for the time being.

He trekked on harder and harder, now all those details of the day of his departure coming back to him as fresh as if he'd only been gone since yesterday. And his mind, somehow, and stubbornly, got itself stuck on those remembrances of Hildie.

Of her soft lips.

That slight scent of ash that always clung to her.

And the gentle, low quality of her voice, that quality that Lou liked to believe was a form of imitation of her father, Ma'reygar, although he'd never met the man.

Hoped never to meet the man.

When Lou saw the first of the canvas rooftops, his feet seemed to scuttle out from beneath him, and he could hardly prevent his forward trajectory. He was bounding down the dirt slope, feeling the puff of dirt all around him, breathing it in, and coughing it out just as quickly.

Everything looked just as it had before, everything in order. And he began to wonder whether he'd been too hasty, if he'd been too foolhardy in returning so suddenly, and on such a whim. What might he have achieved with a few more weeks at Auch'ray's side?

He might've at least learned how to make a protective charm on a consistent basis.

He trod on faster, harder, and he felt his footing give way more than once, but he somehow retained his balance through pure force of will. And soon he was among the tents, hearing the canvas beat in the breeze coming off the Sable Mountains, and he could smell the smoke from a cooking fire, and all the scents that went along with it.

And he felt his stomach rumble.

Lou put his needs aside for a moment, and pressed his mind to the matter at hand. He had to find Hildie, and as quickly as possible.

He *had* to put his mind at rest.

~

Lou passed through the various tents, the ones located around the one he called his own. First of all he looked in on his tent, and glanced around its interior, illuminated with a strange, almost saintly light in the afternoon sun, and found it empty.

But what had he expected?

Hildie to be lurking in the corner, a smirk on her lips, ready to slip a dagger between his ribs?

He pushed on, going to the tent alongside his own. To his sis's tent. To Syre's tent.

Her tent was just as empty as his own, and he felt his nerves draw taut, and his heart tap harder and faster. For the first time since he'd returned he really felt his panic setting in, that his gut feeling had been right all along, that he'd made absolutely the right decision to return when he had.

And then, just over his shoulder, he heard that familiar voice. That *all*-too familiar voice.

"Lou? You're back."

Hildie.

26

FACING A FOE

LOU COULD HARDLY contain the rage which battered against his chest as he turned round. He immediately slipped his hand down his side and felt for the Webbing Blade there. He felt the familiar tickle of its ice magic against his fingertips, and the rage stirring into a tight ball, coming to the point of being uncontrollable.

And then it came in a long, unstoppable, unrelenting wave. And he felt Hildie's fire magic drift over him, much like those waves of heat in Auch'ray's cottage. But now, rather than act to repel him, to repel him and Hildie from one another, it only served to incense him further.

He managed, somehow, to get the words out between his gritted teeth, and his tone was seething with fury. "Where is she?"

For the first time, even with his rage bubbling through him, Lou really saw Hildie. And he saw that her eyes were wide, lips slightly parted, and that she was backing away from him.

She was *frightened*.

And Lou was glad.

"Lou?" she said. "I . . . I didn't expect you back so soon."

"Where. Is. She?" Lou repeated.

Hildie backed up even further, until her back was pressed up against the inside wall of Syre's tent, and he saw that her arms dangled down at her sides.

Defenceless.

Now was his opportunity. He could kill her right now. He had done it before, hadn't he? He knew that he was capable. All he had to do was unsheathe the Webbing Blade and stick her in the gut. That was what she deserved, wasn't it?

Hadn't she once asked him to kill her?

He would be doing her, and the world, a favour.

But he stood his ground, for the time being. He had to remain calm, just long enough to get the answer to his question. "Tell me where she is, right now!"

Hildie's eyes darted about the tent, perhaps looking for some weapon, and Lou knew then that she was afraid to use her magic, that she *feared* using her magic with him. She had no idea just how well Auch'ray had taught him . . . as far as she was concerned, Lou was now a fully fledged ice mage.

And one who now held two of the three magical artefacts, because he was certain she had noted the Webbing Bow which he had slung over his back.

Lou felt his breath come hard and fast, out through his nostrils, and he imagined himself as something approaching a raging bull, surely red in the face from his travels through the Mountains, and the dirt from today's journey still sticking to his skin.

Hildie finally found her voice. "I . . . I"—her Adam's apple bobbed in her sleek, pristine, white-fleshed throat, and a strand of her red hair dangled over her left eye—"You must understand that what I've been doing . . . what I've been doing here, with your people. It's *imperative*, it's the only way they can possibly survive. This is the world we live in, can't you see that? They have to learn to protect themselves. Please, Lou, I—"

But before she could utter so much as another syllable, Lou lurched forwards, hearing the tread of his boots scrape across the dirt floor, and without so much as a conscious thought, his arm leapt out from him, and he seized her about the throat.

He felt his fingers embed themselves there, in her buttery skin, and he could feel the warmth of her fire magic, stirring in her veins, beginning to resist him. And his own heart lodged up in his throat as he asked the question again.

"Where *is* she?!"

He only realised how tightly he held her throat when he realised how reedy her voice came, how impossible to comprehend. And he slackened his grip just enough to allow the words to sneak between her lips.

"Out on the plains." She gasped. "They're out on the plains. With Sully. And Rut. Training. That's what they've been doing. *Training*. Getting ready for the battle."

Lou tightened his hold on her throat, and he felt within himself, quite distinctly, that his ice magic was all building to the very surface of his skin, as if forming icicles that were ready to burst right out, and to cut into *her* skin.

And it was then that he knew he was stronger.

That he could *destroy* her if he wished.

But first he had to find Syre, bring her back to safety.

As he released Hildie, he spun round Syre's tent, taking in the interior. He looked to her bedroll, to the blanket neatly tucked into it, in that very tidy way she had about her. And then he looked to that book which lay beside her bedroll. The one which she had drawn out of their home, back in Endmere, before it had burned to the ground.

The one which Syre had kept with her as a means of comfort.

A Practical Understanding of Dark Magic.

He cast his glare back in Hildie's direction, and he felt the air inside of his lungs cool, and yet tighten at the same time.

Hildie now lay crumpled on the ground, her knees drawn up to her chest, and her head squeezed between her kneecaps. Her back was pressed up against the side of the tent canvas, and he could hear muffled sobs coming from her, and watched as her shoulders shuddered with each one.

"Now I understand," Lou said. "I understand just what you've been planning, just what you've had in mind." He found a sneer sneaking its way onto his lips, and there was no way for him to blunt the edge on his words. "One mage was never going to be enough for you . . . not enough *safety*, in any case. You wanted *her* on your side too."

Hildie just maintained her same posture, still sobbing away, just like the weak, little girl that she had always been. Finding out that her petty squabbles had caught up with her.

"I should kill you," Lou said, and immediately felt the prong of his words jab him in the gut, knowing now that he could no longer take them back.

Now they were said.

Hildie just remained where she was, shaking a touch, no doubt waiting for him to do just as he'd promised, and Lou was of half a mind to do it.

But he didn't.

He held back.

His eyes lingered over that severed left hand of hers, and he thought about the very charm which Auch'ray had taught him, one of those that Lou had in fact managed quite well. One of the *few* Lou had managed. If he wished he could heal her, right here, and right now.

But he wouldn't.

Not yet, anyway.

And he beat his way out of the tent, and back out into the evening sky looming outside.

Off to save Syre.

27

TRAINING ON THE PLAINS

LOU FLED THROUGH THE TENTS, brushing up against the canvas as he went. He could feel the Webbing Bow rocking back and forth between his shoulder blades, and the Webbing Blade's chill at his thigh.

He rushed up through the foothills, and back towards the plains. This was the same way he had gone when he'd rushed off to rescue Sully and Rut, and he was after them again.

While he couldn't quite get round to admitting it to himself, he knew that Sully and Rut had betrayed him as much as Hildie. Although they hadn't so much as laid out an explicit agreement between them, about keeping Syre safe, he'd assumed that they'd be able to see sense for themselves.

In some way he had hoped they'd feel somewhat indebted to Lou, considering he was the one who'd prevented them being carried off to Onderswort, and to never being heard from again. But, he supposed, gratitude often had a strange way of expressing itself.

He reached the top of the foothills, and rose to the position which looked out across the rolling plains below, and he felt his heart wedged in his throat, and his stomach somewhat unsteady. He held his hand over his eyes, shielding them from the bright sun just skimming the horizon now, preparing to drop them into another night.

And Lou could feel the ice purging through his veins, growing more solid, stronger, and he knew that soon he would be walking through the moonlight, and he would be back to full strength. His magic would be striding over its natural domain.

But what good would magic do if he couldn't find Syre?

He continued to scan the plains before him, growing more uneasy as he did so. He tried to pierce the twilight with his vision, but the night was rolling in fast. And he wondered whether he might be better served returning to the encampments, and waiting for Syre there.

But, he thought to himself, and the feeling came up at him from the pit of his stomach, he couldn't trust himself not to run the Webbing Blade through Hildie's neck. He wasn't sure whether or not he had the self control.

He had to walk out here, get as far away as he could from her, and think on the circumstances.

Hopefully, when he returned, he would see things more clearly.

He would see just what needed to be done.

And then, out there in the gloom, he saw movement. He paused, scanned it again and again. Yes, he could see several shapes, *people*, all shuffling towards him, over the plains. He could see a pair of horses with them too. And, as his eyes focussed, grew more accustomed to the twilight, he was sure that he saw Syre mounted upon one of the horse's backs.

His sis.

He had found her.

Lou rushed down the hillside, hearing his feet pounding against the slightly moist earth. A couple of times his boots picked out rabbit holes, and he took care not to trip, not to stumble over and break a bone, because gods knew he needed all his senses about him, he needed every muscle and every bone in pristine condition.

He reached the part of the land where the hill flattened out, and he ran onwards, over the stodgy ground, feeling the long grass brush against the leg of his trousers, and he remained fixed on his target, on the form mounted on horseback, the person he was sure to be Syre.

He ran and ran, feeling the Webbing Bow shifting in its place between his shoulder blades, and the Webbing Blade about its sheath. He would protect her now. He would never dream of leaving her side again. She needed him with her *always*.

She was the only family he had left.

And as Lou padded closer and closer, he noted that the group had halted their procession, and that they held their crossbows up, rigid in their arms.

Didn't they recognise him?

Lou slowed down, but didn't stop his forward motion. He knew that they would recognise him if only he drew a little closer.

And then other thoughts and insinuations struck him.

What if Hildie *had* somehow poisoned them against him? What if she'd told them that Lou had become corrupted with the magic in his veins, and rushed off swearing that he would return one day to slaughter them all?

The possibilities spun through Lou's mind, and he felt his whole body jerk to a halt. When he spoke, his voice was somewhat muffled, unbelieving, and yet he did his best to project his voice through the night air, through the mist rolling in, down over the hills, and threatening to smother the land.

"Don't you recognise me?" Lou called out.

The figures remained just where they stood, about thirty paces from him, their weapons raised, and pointed right at him.

Lou glared at them all, feeling that rage rise back inside of him, even though he knew it was directed at Hildie, that it was her fault.

All of this.

He knew that he had already lost any control he might've had over keeping his rage in check.

And yet, he told himself that he must. Just as Auch'ray had instructed him. That he must embrace weakness, and beware of strength.

But he still reached for the Webbing Bow, over his shoulder, expecting those bolts to come flurrying through the air at any second. And he knew that he had already made peace with death, that he was ready to die. If he couldn't protect them, if they'd turned away from him, if they weren't willing to take him on as their leader, to *allow* him to protect them, then they might as well strike him down right here.

Lou got much further with the Webbing Bow than he would've expected, he now clasped it in his hand, he held tight to the grip and he was fitting an arrow to his string. So it was a surprise when a cry from the group broke the stasis of the scene, ripped through it all like the Webbing Blade through the king's chest.

"Duck!"

28

SCOUTS

LOU DIDN'T HAVE TIME to think. He just did exactly what the voice commanded, and dropped onto his belly, felt the moist earth pass through his cloak and chill his skin. As he lay there, face down on the ground, he wondered why he had obeyed.

Slowly, his conscious mind returned to him, and his mental strength came back to him. He caught onto the realisation gradually, and in patches, knowing just who that voice had belonged to.

Sully.

As Lou lay there on the ground, he listened to the crossbow bolts fling through the air, whizz over his head, and he wondered just what was happening here. If they were firing warning shots at him, just giving him some brutish display of their strength.

Well, if that was all it was, then he might be better off back on his feet. Let them see just what damage their crossbow bolts could do his body, how quickly they could spill his blood. Then they might see how mortal Lou still was.

Back over his shoulder, Lou heard cries.

The cries were coming from the hillside, back off in the direction of the encampments.

A cry for attack.

And Lou knew that the group, those before him, Sully and Rut, and Syre, that they were all firing on the group that was placed behind Lou.

He waited for a gap in the stream of crossbow bolts, and then, when he heard it, he helped himself up to his knees, so that he might see the group first.

Yes, there they all were. Sully. Rut. Other villagers. There must've been two dozen of them, all gathered there. All armed. And then his gaze fell on Syre, on the back of the horse, staring on over Lou's head to the hillside back at the encampments.

And, seemingly with great care, Syre glanced down at Lou, met his eye, and Lou met hers. He felt his stomach stir, and his nerves all sizzle at just the same moment. And he felt his heart lift up in his chest, and a cool wave pass through his blood.

She broke off their gaze, and turned her attention back to the direction in which the others were firing their crossbows.

And Lou looked too.

He saw them, descending the hillside, having come from the direction of the encampments. Ten, or eleven of them. All dressed in cloaks, just like the cloak that he wore. And he instantly knew, from the way that they walked, apparently so calm, unperturbed, that they were mages.

And that they'd come to kill.

Lou thrust himself up off his knees immediately, and he grabbed the Webbing Bow, brought it round, and focussed on those mages advancing on them. Already he could see the protective charm glowing around them, and the crossbow bolts harmlessly bouncing right off the charm, skittering down into the long grass.

If he'd had more presence of mind about him, he might've called for the group to hold their fire. But, as it was, there was simply no time, and so he drew back his arrow and let fly.

He watched the arrow arc through the air, in that beautiful, graceful trajectory that he'd worked on for so long. That had cost him so many hours up there on the mountaintop. And he knew that all that practice had been to serve this one moment.

That this was his opportunity to show his people that he was the protector they required.

The arrow ebbed through the air, and caught the protective charm about midway up its orb. Lou observed the ice magic web out from where the arrowhead had struck, and crack through the entire mass of the protective charm.

And then, just like broken glass, the charm shattered.

Lou realised that the rest of the group *had* stopped firing off their crossbows to watch him take aim with the Webbing Bow. He cast a glance back over them all and, eyes widening, surely like a pair of maddened rat's eyes, he implored them to fire again.

And, after a brief moment of shock, they did.

Their crossbow bolts skittled through the air, and some found their targets. Lou watched them find their targets, and a pair of the cloaked figures advancing on them, now about fifty or sixty paces away, fell to the ground.

The cloaked figures didn't stop to check on their wounded, or their *dead*, they simply continued to advance on them, inching ever closer.

And Lou felt the ice magic prickle through his chest, and he knew that now it was his turn to say the word. "Duck!" he called out, feeling the word sting his throat.

∾

The searing vortex of lightning-blue and fire-red shimmied through the air, and Lou watched it scorch over the plains, racing over the blades of grass as it advanced on them, like a stampeding heard of bulls.

Time again moved slowly, and he knew that the ice magic was possessing him again, that it was giving him a chance. A chance to save his people out here on the plains.

For him to save his sis.

To save Syre.

And this time he knew just what he had to do.

Feeling the moments shift all around him, so slow almost to be imperceptible, he found the words on his lips before he'd had half a chance to think of them, before he'd so much as given them a chance to form in his brain.

And he mumbled them beneath his breath, this time leaving his eyes open, watching that hex hang in the air, that twisted combination of fire and ice magic those mages had cast. The mages that he had no idea where they had come from, let alone why.

But he did know that it was his duty to keep his people from harm.

This wasn't some hailstorm threatening to smash through a couple of panes of glass, or to dislodge some roof tiles, people's lives were on the line.

Now was when it mattered.

And as he felt the words slipping out through his mouth, like honey dribbling past his lips, he felt the ice magic rise up in him, sting him over and over again, almost grow to be unbearable. He knew the magnitude of this task was such that it would take all of his strength, all the strength he had, just to keep the magic flowing, and to somehow channel it into a protective charm.

He felt it build in his solar plexus, and come slowly, and evenly through him. And he felt that familiar tug. The magic grabbing him from his front, and then pulling back out through his spine. He smothered any feeling of failure that might've been lurking in any corner of his mind, and commanded himself to do this right.

This time he *had* to do it right.

As he reached the end of his incantation, coming towards the final phrases of the last stanza of the verse, he couldn't help but notice that there was an echo in his head.

No, another *voice* there.

And he recognised it.

The voice was achingly familiar to him.

With his eyes still open, he shifted his gaze from the advancing hex, from those cloaked figures all marching relentlessly forwards, seemingly unstoppable. And he turned to see Syre, still on horseback, and he watched as her lips traced the exact same words his did.

She too was summoning the protective charm.

Lou couldn't take his eyes off her as he continued to finish the verse, and listened as his words matches hers. He almost didn't have time to register her eyes, to see that whereas before they had been light, and full of life, now they were as black as anything.

Pit-black.

He listened as their words wove together into the twilight air, and he felt that sensation growing within him, at his solar plexus, and he knew what he must do now.

And so he did it.

He let go.

29

A MIGHTY CHARM

THIS TIME the light was so blinding that even when Lou had clamped his eyes shut, and held his arm up to shield his frail eyelids from the glare, he could still feel the sting of the light. He felt the magic lapping all around him, and he thought back to the stream, to that river back in the Sable Mountains, and it reminded him of how the water had stroked his skin.

At his tired limbs.

He felt the magic pelt from his solar plexus in an unstoppable rush, and he knew that this time he had done exactly what was required of him. That he had successfully cast the protective charm.

Or had it been him?

His mind skirted about the possibilities, and thought of Syre, about her muttering along with him, about her speaking the protective charm in time. And then he thought back to the time he'd saved Sully and Rut, and he thought that it was all slipping into place.

Syre was a mage.

Just as he was.

Lou felt his heart tick on, the only sound in his head.

Tick. Tick. Tick, it went.

He could still feel the strength of the charm's glare against his eyelids, causing his still-closed eyes to strain against the light. But he had to know. He had to be sure of it.

And so, feeling the light so bright that it might scorch out his eyeballs, might burn them out completely, he glanced at Syre again, keeping his arm firmly fixed to his forehead in an attempt to keep the worst of the brightness out of his eyes.

Black eyes.

Just *black*.

And he felt something inside of him tickle, some lurching uneasiness. Then he turned his mind back to the matter at hand, and realised that the light was dimming, and that, all around them, the protective charm had set in.

Their protective charm.

Lou's brain was slow to take it all in. He ran his eyes from the base of the protective charm, from its filmy quality, as he'd thought before, just like the bubbles off the surface of a bucket full of soap suds, and he looked up, admiring how it towered up over them, and how it gleamed with a milky quality, like a pearl.

Or, at least, like the pearls he'd seen that the hobblesmen had once brought to their village.

For a few seconds he was lost in it completely and totally, and it was like his whole brain became stamped with that shade, with the beauty of the protective charm. And now he thought to himself that it should've been Syre, and not him, who had gone to receive training from Auch'ray.

He felt the world slowly grinding back into action, and he snapped back to look over their group. Everyone was inside of the bubble, all accounted for. And then he turned his attention to the outside of the bubble. To the cloaked figures. To the *mages* who had hurled the hex at them.

Lou watched the hex continue its approach, now riding towards them through the air at full speed, and he watched as it splashed against the protective charm, like a wave smashing into the beach. And he watched it roll back, and away from them. Its magic dissipating.

Lou reminded himself to breathe. He guessed while he'd been casting the protective charm the thought of breathing had escaped him. And so he gulped down air now, drank it into his lungs, felt it nourish him from the inside out.

He looked back towards the mages and realised that they were still approaching, that they'd done nothing to curtail their advance.

As if looking for the answers, he turned back to look at Syre, and saw that her eyes were still like a pair of coals stuck into her sockets. And that she held still. Her horse, too, Lou noticed, seemed to be struck in a sort of daze, merely swaying from side to side slightly, its head bowed, and apparently unmoved by the spectacle of the protective charm hanging over them.

Ca-kaw!

Ca-kaw!

CA-KAW!

Lou swivelled around, instinctively looking to the sky before he knew just why. And he saw them. That mottled cloud of feathers swirling its way towards them. He thought back to the rescue of Rut and Sully, and he thought about how it had been so similar. That *everything* had been almost exactly the same.

The only difference, Lou supposed, was the scale of the thing.

Whereas before they'd only had to contend with some Royal Guards, this time they were up against several mages. And, as he could see now, Syre was well up to the challenge.

He watched on with the others, from the protective centre of the bubble, as the crows dive-bombed the mages outside. Colours flew from the mages' fingers, and Lou observed several crows, perhaps a hundred or so, simply incinerate in mid-air as the fire magic caught them. But, Lou also saw, that there were perhaps even more crows than before, that they seemed even to outnumber the ones who had swooped down on the gaoler's cart, and picked off all the Royal Guards.

Eaten their flesh.

Looking up about them, Lou could see no sign of the stars above, the crows seemed to have appeared out of thin air, and they were bearing down on the mages.

Lou knew that they'd won when he heard the screeches, when he watched another protective charm rush up about the mages, but far too late. The crows were already inside the charm. There were too many of them.

But that didn't mean that the mages didn't attempt to flee. They did. Scampering off across the plains, with the cloud of crows in pursuit, and with several crows trapped in the protective charm they had cast, now little more than a prison of their own making.

Like the rest of the group, Lou stared off after the mages as they retreated, as they slipped from view, back over the horizon, and away from their immediate thoughts.

And then he turned to Syre, with a million questions on his lips.

30

AN EXPOSED REFUGE

THOSE QUESTIONS, though, would have to wait it seemed. Because, soon after the mages had slipped beyond the horizon, Syre's body was caught in a series of convulsions, and she would've toppled off the saddle and fallen to the ground if it hadn't been for Sully and Rut's quick thinking, catching her between them before she dropped.

Lou guessed that they were there for her. And, contrary to what he'd believed before, about them being the ones protecting Syre, about *him* being the one to protect her, he guessed that it had been her who had been protecting them all along.

But at what cost?

He had rushed over to her, and tried to bring her round from the profound sleep she'd fallen into, but with no luck. She slept on, her chest rising gradually with her gentle breathing. Together, they got her back onto horseback, and led her back to the encampments, where she might be seen by a medicine woman.

Lou hadn't known what to expect, returning to the encampments there. He supposed that he had known the mages must've passed through, that they must've gone there first before turning to the plains. And their presence was made known to him right away when he saw several tents, reduced to smouldering ashes, at the periphery of the encampments.

But, looking around, he saw no more damage.

Or, at least, he couldn't *see* any further damage.

His worries were further laid to rest as they proceeded through the encampments, still dragging Syre's horse along behind them, with Syre collapsed in the saddle. He watched as people came out of their tents, eyes wide, and hair mussed, clearly having passed through something traumatic.

Having come into contact with the mages, was Lou's guess.

But he had no ears to listen to their stories, because they needed to bring their hero—*Syre*—to some much needed medicine.

Lou found the medicine woman in her tent, just as skittish, and with her eyes just as wide as the rest of the people among the encampments. She jabbered away at him about something or other, but Lou soon put her lips to rest when he showed her to Syre, and explained just what they'd been through.

He watched the medicine woman shudder as he explained the part about her black eyes, and he knew, without even asking her the question, what was on her mind.

That Syre had put herself into contact with dark magic.

The medicine woman worked quickly, laying Syre down on the bed she had there, and laying a cool, damp cloth over her head to help soothe her fever. Lou had been surprised when he had brushed Syre's skin and felt her burning up, because he knew, like him, she had ice magic running in her veins. And so, somehow, he had believed her temperature to shift in the other direction.

It just seemed to serve as a reminder of all that he still had to learn about magic, and its effects. In many ways he was still the lowest of the apprentices, though he did have two of the greatest tools of his trade.

The Webbing Bow and the Webbing Blade.

Perhaps he might be better off in handing them over to Syre.

If she pulled through, that was.

The medicine woman soon ushered Lou, and Sully and Rut, who were waiting just outside the medicine woman's tent flap, away from her, telling them that Syre needed some space to breathe. But Lou knew what the real reason was. His mother had been a medicine woman, after all, and although he'd never been present to any dark magic, he knew of the sometimes unpleasant elements that a medicine woman would need to come into contact with to carry out her duties.

And, in a way, he was glad that he wouldn't need to be present.

So, with Sully and Rut at his side, like a pair of faithful old dogs, Lou prowled through the encampments, only now feeling the onrushing effects of tiredness and accumulated fatigue beginning to take hold.

He wished he had something to say to either of them, if he could thank them for looking after Syre, but that had hardly been the case, or if he could press them for more information on just what Hildie had told them.

But the truth was that he was still totally struck dumb by what he had witnessed out on the plains, about the magic his sis had shown. Not just the magic, though, but her *power*. She had great and unmoveable power the like of which he had never experienced and, quite frankly, he never would've believed to exist.

Perhaps the Spider Warrior had shown that level of power.

And then, he felt his chest stir as he thought back to what Auch'ray had said, about having to keep magic in check, and not to allow it to take a person over.

Might that have been what Syre had allowed happen to her?

Had she allowed dark magic to take hold of her?

The more Lou thought about it, the more he realised that there *was* something that he could do. And so, with a look to each Rut and Sully, he left them behind and headed for Syre's tent.

When Lou reached Syre's tent, he felt his nerves jangle, and he knew that it was because he was recalling that same rage he had felt towards Hildie. It was strange now, how his rage had boiled down completely, almost vanished from him. He wondered if it was because he was tired, or because his sis was in a perilous state, or maybe it was because he was realising that Hildie wasn't the real culprit here.

That she had done nothing wrong.

Well, he could seek her out later and get the story straight, once Syre was back on her feet. He guessed he would have some stern words for her considering that she'd allowed Syre to use that dark magic . . . no, *encouraged* her to do so.

And now just look where it had left her.

He knew that out there on the plains, when he had gone off to save Sully and Rut, Hildie hadn't been testing *him*, he hadn't been the one she'd been watching. But she'd kept her eye on Syre— Syre had been what had interested her. And getting Lou out of the encampments had provided Hildie with the opportunity to get her hands on that raw power.

Lou focussed in on the bedroll, and then looked to that hefty tome at her bedside, and he knew just what he had to do.

After snatching up the book, he emerged outside the tent, and he looked to the night sky, to the smoke rising up into the sky, against the swelling moonlight. All those campfires still burning away, apparently oblivious, or indifferent, to the visit of the mages. He studied the smoke, and then picked out where he determined it to be the thickest, and headed in that direction.

The fire crackled hard, and spat out several sparks as Lou approached, as if it knew just what he was determining to feed it. He wondered about the elements, and about magic, and whether or not they did feel. If they were entwined with the fabric of magic throughout the world. And he guessed that was a question for another day.

He looked to a sleepy-eyed man who sat at the fire, roasting his bare feet in the glow. He pursed his lips together and gave Lou a nod, and then turned back to the flames.

Lou felt the ice magic twitch through his veins, as if thawing inside him. He didn't want to stand too close, or for too long. He just wanted to get this unpleasant deed done with and move on. Though the medicine woman wouldn't like it, he wanted to be close to his sis, in case she woke up.

He stared down at the book, at the faded golden lettering there, almost completely rubbed off, Lou guessed, following all its travelling, all its trials and tribulations in Syre's arms.

A Practical Understanding of Dark Magic.

As he drew his arm back and tossed the book onto the flames, he tried not to think of his ma, of how that book had once lined her shelves. It made him flinch to think that his ma had ever consulted it.

Why would she ever have needed to consult it?

The book landed onto the pile of burning wood with a slight *slap*, and it lay there, in the heat of the flames for a while without moving, as if the fire was considering whether or not it was going to consume the pages, if it really had the hunger for such a weighty tome.

And in the end Lou saw that it did.

The leather-bound cover melted in the flames, whatever was left of its veneer peeled back, and then the pages started to burn.

Lou wondered if he'd expected the book to burst into green flames, or to spit poison, or to unfurl a hex on the encampment, but nothing happened.

The pages flickered in the flames, and the book was soon devoid of any colour or distinguishing feature, to mark it apart from the logs burning away there.

And Lou was glad.

He simply wanted it to transform into mulch, to be gone forever more from his, and *their*, lives.

The best for all of them.

And then, with a parting nod to the man who had started the fire, Lou shifted off, away from the glare and sting of the firelight, and back to walk among the tents.

Lou was on his way to go and visit Syre when he noted the sound of boot steps behind him. His immediate thought was that it was

Hildie, that she was coming to explain herself to him. But then he established that there were two sets of boots. Two people. And, from the weight of their gait, men.

He turned back, peeling back the gloom with his eyes, peering into the darkness at his heels. There he saw Sully and Rut. His two most faithful companions. His fellow skullers. And to think now that Sully had once been the one to look out for Lou.

Oh, how that had changed.

Like always, it was Rut who spoke, with Sully preferring to slink back into the shadows, not too difficult here in the darkness. And he spoke quickly, fluidly, as if his words might expire if he didn't take care. "Hildie," Rut said.

Just hearing her name sent tingles running down Lou's spine, but when he answered he noted that his voice sounded weary. "What about her?"

Rut shook his head a couple of times, and blinked too, as if struck by some sort of disbelief.

"What is it?" Lou said, feeling himself growing irritated by the suspense.

If she wanted to meet him on a level playing field, if she wanted to invite him to kill her again, then she might find him willing to carry out the act. If she pushed him hard enough.

"She's gone," Rut said.

Lou felt the tension ebb out of his muscles, and only then realised that he *had* been tense about the whole thing, that he'd been in suspense over just what had gone on with her. And he knew then that he did care . . . and more, that he would *never* be capable of killing her.

At least he couldn't see his way to doing so.

Rut continued, "I spoke to some of the people, those who were back here at the encampments, they told me about how the mages arrived, how they were freezing tents, setting some ablaze, muttering all kinds of strange incantations."

Lou wanted Rut to cut to the chase, he needed to get back to Syre's side and soon. If she woke up he wanted to be by her side, ready to take her hand in his own. He certainly didn't want her to wake up with only a stranger for company, even if that stranger was a medicine woman.

"Then Hildie," Rut went on, "she cast a protective charm over the whole of the encampments, sealed the whole place in a bubble, she warded the mages off."

Lou felt his heart drop down to his stomach, and his toes went numb. He allowed the words Rut had just spoken to tumble round his mind a while, and then he realised that Rut *had* said what he'd just said. And that, according to his claim, Hildie had *saved* the people here.

Was that really how it was?

Lou now felt himself drowning in remorse, thinking back to his bloody-minded thoughts on what he might do to her, that he might be prepared to kill her. What about the last man he had killed? He had hardly had a nightmare-free night since he had done so, and so what would another murder do to his soul?

His mind spun back to the bridge, to the day when she'd wished him off into the Sable Mountains, that kiss they'd shared, and how he had thought of nothing else seemingly for weeks. And he knew that, whatever else passed between them, they were special to one another.

His heart wrenched in his chest as he thought back to the first thing Rut had said, and he turned back to him, a new sharpness in his glare. "And where did she go?"

Rut pouted and then shrugged, turning up his palms. "No idea, no one knows. Once she saw off the mages she simply disappeared. Someone said they saw her headed up the path, up into the Sable Mountains, but who really knows the truth? Maybe she'll be back later?"

Lou thought that over too, about why'd she decided, having seen off the mages, to take her leave. Then he recalled the scene between the two of them, back in Syre's empty tent, and the fear he'd inspired in her. And he knew the truth, that she'd thought him capable, with his new weapons, of easily overcoming the incoming mages. And once she'd taken care to protect the villagers in the encampments, she'd believed it better to make her disappearance.

Lou jerked his head upwards, to look to the Sable Mountains looming over their heads, as if he might be able to see her up there, see her making her way along the path, perhaps the same one he'd taken, to Ravensbark.

But, of course, all he could see in the moonlight was the outline of the Mountains, and no detail. For all he knew she *was* up there, looking down on them, but he would never be able to see her.

His gut wrenched once again, and he turned back to look over Sully and Rut. He managed a smile, and a well-done clap on the shoulder for each of them. And then he made his way through the tents, back towards the medicine woman's tent.

As Lou neared the tent, he heard voices, voices inside. And he felt a thrill pass through his heart, because he recognised it as his sis's voice. But he held back. He wasn't sure why, but he did, and he listened first to Syre speak.

"My brother?" she said. "Where's my brother?"

"Coming, my dear," the medicine woman replied.

"What . . . what happened?"

The medicine woman slipped into silence for several seconds, and then she said, "Don't you remember?"

"No, nothing."

There was the tinkling of glass, perhaps of medicine decanters the woman kept there, and the shuffling of feet moving over the tent floor. Lou could picture the medicine woman inside, trying to make Syre drop the topic altogether.

He knew how hard it must be for her.

And so, just then, Lou chose his moment to slip in through the tent flap, to enter the medicine woman's tent.

First of all he took in the medicine woman herself, standing with her back to him, still tinkling away with whatever glass equipment she had there. She turned her head so her face was in profile to him. "You can see your sister now," she said.

But already Lou had turned his attention to the bed, to his sister propped up in her bed, and her eyes just about peering out from beneath her drooping eyelids.

Lou felt his heart jolt in his chest, and he rushed forwards to kneel down at her side. He took her hands in his and felt those nimble, fragile fingers of hers in his. And, he was sure, that same tickle of ice magic dancing through her veins, still settling down after its stellar appearance only hours earlier.

"How do you feel?" Lou said.

Syre eyed him, seemingly from the backs of her eyes, and he noted that it seemed like she had bruising about her eye sockets, as if she'd had several sleepless nights. She spoke in a low, weak voice, but all her words were clear. "I feel fine," she said.

"Good," Lou said, unable to keep from smiling. "That's great."

And then her eyes seemed to bounce into life, her eyeballs got larger and explored his. "Tell me, Lou, what happened to me?"

Lou reached out and patted the back of her hand and smiled more easily, already feeling his heart lightening, and the prickle of the ice magic in his veins begin to subside, to calm down. "It's okay," he said. "We've got plenty of time. The most important thing now is you get some rest."

"What about Hildie? Where's Hildie?"

Again, Lou felt his gut twist, but this time there was no anger, no boiling rage somehow suppressed inside him. And he managed to keep up his smile. "Hildie," he said. "We can talk about Hildie once you've had some rest."

"Can I see her, will she come to visit me?"

He patted her hand once more, still surprised by her delicate flesh as compared to her astonishing power. "We'll see about that," he said. "We'll see."

31

THE MAGICAL COUNCIL VOTES

MA'REYGAR SAT UPRIGHT in the hard wooden chair in his quarters, and he stared at the candle flickering before him on the desk. He watched as a bead of wax rolled down the candlestick before splattering onto the desk itself.

He reached out and held his hand over the freshly dropped wax. He could still feel the heat coming off it, feel the fire magic responding to it within his palm. And then, for what must've been the thousandth time that evening, he glanced back out the window to the front steps of the Magical Council, to those grey, stone slabs that led up to the entrance hall.

No sign of them yet.

Still.

Ma'reygar shifted from his chair, and stomped about his room. He marched from one side to the other, back and forth, again and again. He had been cooped up here for weeks now, in the Magical Council, and he was beginning to suspect that there might be some form of treachery afoot.

Would Yunt'ga'boar dare?

Ma'reygar supposed, if Yunt'ga'boar did intend to dispose of him then the Magical Council would be the place to do it. He would have six other mages to call upon, to help him out. But if he did intend to *assassinate* him, or whatever, then why hadn't he done it already?

During one of these asinine weeks.

Ma'reygar trudged back up to the window and stared out once more. They had been gone for almost a month now. That scout group.

After his proposal, his bringing information about the Kingdom of Shellacnass's intentions to move in on the Sable Mountains, to drive magic from the kingdom once and for all, Yunt'ga'boar, the rest of the Council for that matter, had got all aflutter with activity.

They had taken his claims seriously.

And why shouldn't they have?

Hadn't *he*, Ma'reygar, been the one who had stopped the dreaded Spider Warrior? The one, all things being fair, who should really be the High Chair of the Magical Council?

But there was little point in petty contemplation, the time had now come for action. And if he was to have his vengeance, if he was to be given the Council's blessing, and their support, in his wish to overthrow Ilsnare, he would be contented with being made King of Shellacnass.

Yes, that would be a fair consolation prize.

A magical king for a mortal realm, what could be better?

Already he could almost see himself in that throne room, that goose-feather, velvet cushion beneath his backside, and that sceptre in his hand . . . or whatever it was the king carried these days.

There wouldn't be any disobedience in his kingdom, that was for certain, from mortal *or* mage alike.

Ma'reygar continued to stare out the window. He was sure that he saw something there, something *beyond* the gloom. Shapes. People. Moving through? Or was it just his imagination. He had been waiting so long now, and he could almost feel himself shaking with anticipation. In fact, yes, looking at his hand he saw it shaking.

Further to Ma'reygar's report, the scout group, a select party of mages, had been sent to investigate the circumstances of the Kingdom of Shellacnass, and to gauge their progress towards the Sable Mountains.

Though Ma'reygar had been fairly certain that Yunt'ga'boar wouldn't take his word at face value, that he would almost certainly send out a collection of his own eyes and ears, he had been profoundly annoyed when it had actually happened.

Because it showed everyone, the whole *damn* Council, that Yunt'ga'boar didn't trust him an inch. Thinking about it, Ma'reygar knew that no one on the Council really trusted him. It was all over that Webbing Blade business, his being given it by Auch'ray. He knew that was the source of their distrust.

Imbeciles.

But let them try to find it. His daughter would keep it close, keep it safe, keep it hidden.

Forever.

For now, though, everything was in their hands.

Ma'reygar had already been making contingency plans, if the scouting group returned to inform of the Council that Ma'reygar had been lying. But he hoped it wouldn't come to that. Those dark ages of blood and guts and hexes had seemed long passed.

Although they *had* proved effective at achieving their ends.

He stared deeper into the gloom out his window, through the frosty pane, the pane he was sure that Yunt'ga'boar took extra special care to keep especially chilly just for Ma'reygar, such was his jealousy of his power.

That was fine, though. Let them be jealous. Ma'reygar would have the last laugh, like always.

Yes, he could see them out there, the mages. The *scouts*. Returning from their mission, ready to bring ill or fortune . . . for one or the other, for him, or for Yunt'ga'boar.

Ma'reygar felt himself quiet down within himself. He felt the fire magic settle in his veins, and lie dormant for a while. Yes, he had to be calm and ready for whatever news came his way.

So that he had the energy to take whatever course of action required taking.

Ma'reygar guessed an hour or more had gone by before he heard the *scuffle* of footsteps outside his chamber door. He propped himself back up in his chair and returned to the book he'd been leafing through, to give the appearance of a mage at work . . . and very much *unconcerned* as to the outcome of the scouting mission.

A knock at his door.

"Come in."

A younger mage there, Ma'reygar forgot his name, peeped in from the hall. "Sir, the Council is ready to deliver its verdict."

Its verdict, already?

Ma'reygar couldn't quite believe it. Sure, he wasn't a member of the Council, and he really had no official standing, but he'd been almost certain that they'd at least extend him the courtesy of letting him know the outcome of the scouting mission *before* they voted.

But he calmed himself. Reminded himself that whatever the outcome *he* would be the victor. Because, as the whole world knew, he was the mightiest mage. They all feared him. And if they wished to all take him on, well . . . they would see who would come out best.

The vote being taken quickly meant only one thing, though, Ma'reygar thought to himself as he skirted the heels of the younger mage as he padded round the labyrinthine corridors. It meant that the scouting group had found *conclusive* evidence that Ma'reygar had been lying, and they'd decided *not* to action against the mortals.

Ma'reygar gripped his staff tight in his fist, knowing just what he was going to hurl first, how he would take the pre-emptory strike. Because, if he knew nothing else, he knew all of these mages, all of the members of the Council, and their magic, inside out.

They were predictable to him, and that was why only *he* had been able to stop the Spider Warrior. *He* had been the only one able to outsmart that most pure of ice magic. And here they were, thinking that he was just a doddery old mage that could brushed under the carpet . . . just like they'd done with Auch'ray, perhaps the only man in this world he could really describe as 'friend.'

He could already feel the heat of the meeting hall fire, and it only served to energise him further. He drew on its strength, it built him up, flexed his muscles, and now, all that remained was for him to release that brute force, to bring it down on the Council.

And then all of their charges, all the mages who looked to the Council for guidance, all the hundreds—or were there thousands now?—of mages would yield to him, and he would have his army at last.

The younger mage, perhaps sensing the ferocity of Ma'reygar's magic in the air, glanced back briefly over his shoulder.

That was right. That *boy* he would be his servant, just like the rest of the magical community.

Ma'reygar pressed his lips tight together as they rounded the corner and entered the meeting hall. There they all were:

Kwar.

Ems'plot.

Lumbswich.

Grendlin.

J'plaut.

Wyd'rswen.

And, last but not least . . . at least not *yet* . . . Yunt'ga'boar, at the head of the table.

Already Ma'reygar had his hexes etched on his mind, and he thought of his direction of attack. That he would start with the ice mages. He had always harboured the feeling that he would be able to defeat them quickly, painlessly.

The fire mages would take more work.

And he wished to leave Yunt'ga'boar until last, because he had to suffer. He had to know the *pain* of his mistake.

Ma'reygar prepared himself, the incantations flowed as a part of him, and he turned his attention to that old imposter Yunt'-ga'boar and awaited his speech.

Yunt'ga'boar slowly got to his feet, brushing the parchment before him to one side, and replacing his quill into its respective inkwell. Today he wore a turquoise cloak which hugged his slithery frame. "We have voted on the matter, Ma'reygar," he said.

Ma'reygar gripped his staff a little tighter, and he felt a tiny spark burst from one of his fingertips. He gazed about the table, sure one of the Council must have noticed, but all their faces were still blank.

Blank as stone.

Ma'reygar tilted his chin up in a regal fashion, like the king he was soon to be.

"We have voted in favour of building an army and leading it against the mortals."

Ma'reygar's heart rammed right up to his throat, and he felt himself swallowing the incantation, taking it right back down. His whole body, it had been so prepared, he had been primed for the answer . . . for the *other* answer, but it hadn't come.

Slowly it began to sink in, and Ma'reygar realised that he had won.

That he would have his war.

His *vengeance*.

And he resisted every urge in his body screaming out for him to unfurl the greediest and most satisfied of grins upon the Council. He stood his ground, awaiting Yunt'ga'boar's explanation.

Yunt'ga'boar, his hair a little ragged now that Ma'reygar took in his aspect properly, and his eyes etched with rings, continued, "Contrary to your claims, the scouts failed to find any sign of an advancing mortal army, one making headway into the Sable Mountains." He glanced over the table to another of the mages, Ma'reygar couldn't care less which one. "They did *however* proceed to Ilsnare, and carried out an espionage operation in the city." He glanced up, momentarily meeting Ma'reygar's eye, but quickly looking away. "And they discovered that the king has been murdered."

Ma'reygar felt a pang hit his heart. The king? Murdered? And how had this tender morsel escaped his attention? Sure, he supposed that he had been off in the wildness for some time now, with his head to the ground, but why wouldn't such large piece of news catch his ear somewhere?

Slowly the implications sunk in for him, and already, before Yunt'ga'boar finished his missive, Ma'reygar knew exactly what he had to say.

Yunt'ga'boar continued, "The new head of state, as per protocol, while a suitor may be found, is the Captain of the Royal Guards." Once more his eyes flitted about the table before he added, "Herimyre."

Ma'reygar could feel the tension taut in the air, and he knew the fear that name imposed on the members of the Council here, that name that'd made them run to the Sable Mountains, their tails between their legs. Well now, they had to stand up and they had to fight.

There would be no other way.

Yunt'ga'boar continued, "Given Herimyre's past policy towards the magical community it has been agreed, and voted on, that we should commence building an army right away, an army which can counteract any such strike which Herimyre might be planning."

Ma'reygar felt the satisfaction open within his chest, and his fire magic bubbling away delightfully in his veins. Today would surely be marked in history for all time.

What a wonderful, spectacular day!

But it seemed Yunt'ga'boar had one more item to add, since his eyes continued to linger over Ma'reygar somewhat unsteadily. "Ma'reygar, the Council has called you before it today to make a request."

Ma'reygar felt the bubbling of fire magic subside a moment, the edge of his thrill become blunt. He grasped hold of his staff once more and prepared himself for the worst. If *anything* came between himself and Herimyre now, he would rain hell down upon them all.

Yunt'ga'boar flinched and then said, "The Council would be glad to know whether you would be willing to lead the magical army in this war."

And then delight swamped in over Ma'reygar, and seemed to consume him whole. It took just about all his inner strength to utter the words, to get them out before the Council.

"Why," he said, "it would be my *greatest* pleasure."

AUTHOR'S NOTE

Thank you for taking the time to read one of my books. If you would like to hear about my latest releases you can sign up for my newsletter here: www.raymondsflex.com

Thanks for reading!

Raymond S Flex

The Webbing Bow
The Second Crystal Kingdom Novel

Copyright © Raymond S Flex, 2014.
Published by DIB Books
All rights reserved.

Cover design and layout copyright © DIB Books, 2014.
Cover art copyright © Andriy Zholudyev & Mopic / Shutterstock, 2014.